D0185377

truong

THE SCAPEGOAT

"Here is writing as pleasure, narrative that moves along at a fine pace . . . Here is life, with its ration of unpredictability that insists on cropping up where you least expect it"

PIERRE MAURY, *Magazine Littéraire*

"A real lark, you'll laugh till you cry . . . a crime novel in a class of its own . . . an unlikely marriage between a children's story and a thriller"

BERTRAND AUDUSSE, *Le Monde*

"Already one of the top names in crime fiction"

JEAN-PIERRE MOGUI, *Figaro*

"Pennac takes delight in being the most meticulous of writers"

JEAN-PIERRE GONGUET, *Matin*

"An author who writes gleefully and loads the texts with images and metaphors"

LOUIS DESTREM, *Humanité*

"Above all it's the ebullient, scintillating style, pert and syncopated, a veritable cascade of fireworks"

JEAN CLÉMENTIN, *Canard Enchaîné*

DANIEL PENNAC was born in Casablanca in 1944, his father being in the French colonial service. In his youth he travelled widely in Europe, Asia and Africa, and has been employed in a number of capacities, including woodcutter, Paris cab driver, illustrator and schoolteacher. His four novels written round the character of Benjamin Malaussène, the professional scapegoat, have been published in many languages. He has also written a book out of his experience teaching young children, which has been published in English as *Reads like a Novel*. He is married, with one child.

IAN MONK is one of the most resourceful translators from French. He made his own translation of Georges Perec's e-less novel *La Disparition* before Harvill published Gilbert Adair's version, and went on to translate Perec's novella that uses no vowel but e, *Les Revenentes*, which was published by Harvill in a volume with two other Perec translations by his hand, *Three by Perec*. He has also translated the Corto Maltese cartoon strips by Hugo Pratt. A long-time resident of Paris, he is well acquainted with the local idiom.

Also by Daniel Pennac in English translation

READS LIKE A NOVEL

THE FAIRY GUNMOTHER

WRITE TO KILL

Daniel Pennac

THE SCAPEGOAT

Translated from the French by
Ian Monk

THE HARVILL PRESS
LONDON

To "Le Gros"
To Robert Soulat

First published with the title *Au Bonheur des ogres* by Editions Gallimard, 1985

First published in Great Britain by the Harvill Press in 1998

This paperback edition first published in 1999 by
The Harvill Press, 2 Aztec Row, Berners Road, London N1 0PW

www.harvill-press.com

1 3 5 7 9 8 6 4 2

A CIP catalogue record for this book is available from the British Library

This translation is published with the financial
assistance of the French Ministry of Culture

ISBN 1 86046 611 7

Designed and typeset in Minion at
Libanus Press, Marlborough, Wiltshire

Printed and bound in Great Britain by Mackays of Chatham

Half title: Illustration by Marcelino Truong

To lure little Dionysus into their circle, the Titans shook various sorts of rattles at him. Attracted by these bright objects, the child walked towards them and the monstrous circle closed around him. The Titans then killed Dionysus together; after which they cooked and devoured him.

RENÉ GIRARD, *Le Bouc Emissaire*

. . . the faithful hope that if only the saint is present . . . then he will be struck down instead of them. RENÉ GIRARD, *Le Bouc Emissaire*

The wicked at heart probably know something. WOODY ALLEN

Chapter 1

A FEMALE VOICE emerged from the loudspeaker, as airy and full of promise as a bridal veil:

"Monsieur Malaussène is requested at the Customer Complaints Office."

It was a misty voice, as if a David Hamilton photo'd just opened its mouth. But, all the same, there was still a detectable smirk lurking behind Miss Hamilton's haze. And the smirk wasn't a nice one at all. Anyway, I had to go. I reckoned I might make it there by this time next week. It was four fifteen p.m. on December 24 and the Store was at bursting point. A densely packed army of customers laden with goodies was jamming the aisles. It was a glacier imperceptibly inching its way forwards, solid with unseen pent-up energy. There were fixed grins, gleaming sweat, silent cussings, daggered looks and terrified screams from children being kidnapped by cotton-wool Santas.

"Don't be frightened, darling, it's Father Xmas!"

Flashes flashed.

As for Father Xmas, I could see one, who was massive and translucent, dominating that motionless crush with his terrible, cannibalistic looks. His mouth was a cherry. His beard was white. His smile was lovely. He had children's legs dangling out from between his lips. It was Half Pint's latest drawing at school. His teacher had pulled quite a face. "Do you reckon it's normal for a child his age to draw a Father Xmas like that?" "And what about Father Xmas, then?" I snapped back. "Do you reckon he's that *normal* himself?" I picked Half Pint up in my arms. He was running one hell of a temperature. He was so hot that his glasses had misted over, which made him squint even more than usual.

"Monsieur Malaussène is requested at the Customer Complaints Office."

Monsieur Malaussène heard you, for fuck's sake! He had even reached the bottom of the main escalator. And he'd be on his way up it by now, if he hadn't been glued to the spot by the dark eye of a cannon. Because I was the person the bastard was aiming at. No doubt about it. The turret had swivelled round, settled itself in my direction, then the cannon had raised its muzzle till it was pointing straight between my eyes. The turret and the cannon belonged to an AMX 30 tank, under the remote control of a four-foot-eight-inch tall oldster who was chuckling away contentedly to himself. It was one of Theo's countless little old men. Only this one was really little, and prodigiously old, and easily identifiable thanks to the grey smock Theo had them all wear so as to keep tabs on them.

"For the last time, granddad, put that toy back!"

The salesgirl wearily nagged at him from behind the toy counter. She looked like a lovely little squirrel with its cheeks full of hazelnuts. With his thumb on the firing button, the old lad spat out a childish refusal. My heels clicked impeccably to attention and I said:

"The AMX 30 is no longer in service, Colonel. It's only good for the scrap heap or for some banana republic."

The little oldster glanced sadly down at his plaything then, with a despairing hand, motioned me to go on. The salesgirl smiled at me as if she was awarding me a gerontologist's diploma. Cazeneuve, the floor detective, burst out of the woodwork and furiously grabbed hold of the tank.

"You really do always have to fucking stir it, don't you, Malaussène?"

"Shut it, Cazeneuve!"

The atmosphere mounted . . . Now that his tank was gone, the little oldster stood beating his arms in the air. Feeling rather relieved, I let the escalator whisk me away, like I was hoping for purer air upstairs.

What I ran into upstairs was Theo. Togged out in a flamingo-pink two-piece, he was, as usual, queuing up in front of the photo booth. He smiled sweetly at me.

"Theo, one of your little ones is causing havoc down in the toy department."

"So what? Just as long as he doesn't start flashing outside schools."

My smile met his. Then Theo winked across at the glass cage containing the Customer Complaints Office.

"Looks like they're onto your case in there."

Too bloody right. It only took me a second to figure out that Lehmann had already been at it for quite a while. He was explaining to one of our lady customers how it was all my fault. Tears were bursting out in short spurts from her eyes. She'd parked her pudgy baby in the corner, crammed forcibly into its shoddy old buggy. I opened the door. And I heard Lehmann declare in a tone of heart-felt sympathy:

"I couldn't agree with you more, madam. It's absolutely unacceptable. In fact . . ."

He'd spotted me.

"In fact, here he is. We'll ask him what he thinks about it."

His voice had changed registers. It had gone from the understanding to the venomous. It was an open and shut case. Lehmann laid it before me with hypnotic precision. The pudgy baby stared at me with the sweetest face in the world. So, three days before, my department had supposedly sold this very lady a refrigerator of such a huge capacity that she had therein stashed a Xmas feast fit for twenty-five people, trimmings and afters included. Then, for some reason which Lehmann wanted me to provide, this fridge had suddenly transformed itself into an incinerator. When our lady customer had opened it that morning, it had been a miracle that she hadn't been burnt to a cinder. I glanced across at her. It was true. Her eyebrows were a bit singed. The pain which could be felt lurking behind her anger helped me look pathetic. The baby was staring at me as if it was all down to me. My own eyes looked anxiously across at Lehmann who, with his arms crossed, leant back against the edge of his desk and said:

"Well, we're waiting."

Silence.

"Quality control is your department, isn't it?"

I nodded my head in agreement and stammered out how right he was, and how that was just why the whole thing beat me, what with all the tests we'd carried out . . . Just like last week's gas cooker or that law firm's Hoover!

The tiddler's eyes were clearly saying that I was the one behind the clubbing to death of baby seals. Lehmann turned back to the customer. He spoke to her as if I wasn't even there, thanking her for putting in such a strongly worded complaint. (Outside, Theo was still hanging round in front of the photo booth. I remembered that I'd have to ask him to give me one of his snaps for Half Pint's album.) Lehmann was now into explaining how it was the clientele's responsibility to help clean up the world of business. It went without saying that her guarantee would be respected and that the Store would at once provide her with another refrigerator.

"As for the other material damages of which you and your loved ones have been victims," (he spoke like that, did our ex non-commissioned officer Lehmann, with, at the back of his throat, a hint of his good old Alsace, where he'd been dropped off by the stork – which had been fuelled up on Riesling.) "Monsieur Malaussène will be pleased to make them good. At his own personal expense, of course."

Then he added:

"Merry Xmas, Malaussène!"

When Lehmann started into retracing my career in the Store, when he started explaining how, thanks to her, that career was now drawing to a close, what I could read in that lady's weary eyes was first embarrassment, then compassion, with tears welling back up and soon fluttering on the tips of her lashes.

That's it, the time was now ripe for me to get my own tear ducts functioning. Which I did, while turning my face away. Through the bay window, I stared down into the maelstrom of the Store. A relentless heart was pumping even more corpuscles into those clotted-up arteries. It was like the whole human race was struggling underneath a vast sheet of wrapping paper. Beautifully translucent balloons were constantly rising up from the toy department and gathering together in clumps, trapped by the frosted glass ceiling. Daylight filtered through those multi-coloured clusters. How beautiful. The customer was trying in vain to butt in while Lehmann was mercilessly drawing up my CV to come. It wasn't looking good. I was heading for a couple of two-bit jobs, then the sack once more, an endless wait in the dole queue, the doss house and finally a pauper's grave. When she looked round at me, I was in tears. Lehmann didn't raise his voice. He just carefully drove the dagger home.

What I could then see in the customer's eyes didn't surprise me at all. *What I could see was herself.* All I'd had to do was burst into tears for her to put herself in my shoes. Compassion. While Lehmann was pausing for breath, she at last managed to get a word in. She took everything back. She was withdrawing her complaint. All she wanted was for us to respect the guarantee for the fridge. There was no need for me to make good that twenty-five-head Xmas dinner. (At some time or another Lehmann must have mentioned my salary.) She'd never forgive herself if she got me sacked on Xmas Eve. (Lehmann had slipped the word "Xmas" in a good twenty times). Anyone could make a mistake. She herself, not long ago, at work . . .

Five minutes later, she left the Customer Complaints Office bearing a voucher for a brand new fridge. The baby and its buggy got stuck for a moment in the door. With a tense sob, she gave it a good shove.

Lehmann and I were left on our own. I glanced at him as he started to piss himself then – suddenly feeling all in – I murmured:

"Right pair of bastards, aren't we?"

His Alsatian jaws opened to answer me. But something slammed them shut.

Something coming up from the guts of the Store.

A muffled explosion. Followed by screaming.

Chapter 2

We pressed our two noses up against the bay window. At first, we couldn't see a thing. Two or three thousand balloons, blown about by the explosion, were blocking our view of the Store. It was only when they started to drift slowly back up towards the light that they revealed to us what I'd rather not have seen.

"Shit," Lehmann muttered.

The customers were in total panic. They were all looking for the exit. The bigger ones were trampling over the smaller ones. Some of them were even dashing directly along the counter tops, splashing socks and knickers all over the shop. Here and there, a sales assistant or security guard was trying to dam up the panic. A hefty character in a violet jacket had been thrown through a cosmetics display case. I opened the Complaints Office's glass door. It was like opening a window in the middle of a typhoon. The Store was one gigantic scream. Next to me, a loudspeaker was trying to calm things down. If we hadn't been in danger of dying of something else, Miss Hamilton's voice would have made us laugh ourselves to death: a scent spray in the midst of a hurricane. It was war down below. While, up above, the balloons had become see-through once again. The entire horror show was being bathed in their incredibly sweet pinkish light. Lehmann came out to join me and barked into my ear:

"Where did it come from? Where did it go off?"

In his veteran's voice, there was a hint of rekindled colonial war excitement. I didn't know where it had gone off. A heap of bodies, bristling with arms and legs, was blocking the escalator. Customers were bounding up the down escalator, only to be pushed back again by the force of the wave coming from above. After a brief exchange of views, they all found themselves at the bottom of the stairs, jammed up against that human stopper. They squirmed and screamed.

"Shit!" Lehmann yelled. "Shit, shit, shit . . ."

Rowing with his elbows, he headed off towards the escalator, dived onto the control panel and switched the thing off.

By the curtain of the photo booth, Theo was holding four versions of his gob up to the light. He was looking pleased. He handed me one of his snaps:

"Here," he said. "For Half Pint's album."

Then things calmed down. Things calmed down because, after all, nothing was happening. Something had exploded somewhere, but nothing had happened next. So, things calmed down. And before long our suave Miss Hamilton could be heard kindly requesting our valued customers to leave the Store in an orderly fashion and for our staff to get back to their posts. And that's exactly what came to pass. The crowd drifted smoothly away towards the exits, leaving behind it a wasteland of abandoned handbags, shoes, multi-coloured parcels and children. I expected to see a good hundred corpses. But I didn't. Here and there, the staff were bending down over dazed customers, who soon got to their feet and hobbled off towards the exits.

A small side door had been reserved for the police. And so that was where they made their entrance. They headed straight off towards the toy department. The toy department! I immediately thought of my little squirrel-faced salesgirl and of Theo's tiny oldster. I leapt down the motionless escalator with a nasty feeling which, like all nasty feelings, turned out to be unwarranted. The stiff was that of a sixtyish-year-old man, who must have been completely gutted, judging by the quantity of ketchup he'd sprayed around the place. The bomb had almost sliced him in half. While honking as discreetly as possible, I thought, God knows why, of Louna. Louna, Laurent and the sprog. She'd now called me up three times: "Some advice, Ben, give me your opinion." What advice could I possibly give to you, my poor darling? Just look at the state of me!

My mind went on the rampage while blankets covered up our splattered customer.

"Not a pretty sight, is it?"

The little copper treated me to a friendly grin. In the state I was in, that was certainly better than nothing. And so it was more or less from gratitude that I answered, aloofly:

"Not really, no."

He nodded his head and went on:

"Well, suicides in the métro are even worse!"

(That was nice to know . . .)

"Blood and guts everywhere, fingers stuck in the axles . . . I know what I'm talking about because, as I'm the smallest in the brigade, I'm always the one that gets lumbered."

He wasn't a copper. He was a fireman. A dark blue fireman with red piping. A really tiny one. A helmet bigger than he was clinked against his belt.

"But the worst thing of all, between you and me, are the first-degree burns in car crashes. You just can't get rid of the stink. It stays in your hair for at least a fortnight!"

There were no more balloons in the sky above the toy department. They'd all been blown away by the blast, way up there, against the glass ceiling. Someone was leading away my little squirrel, who was sobbing. The fireman pointed at the wrapped-up body:

"Did you notice something odd? He had his flies open!"

(No, as a matter of fact I didn't.)

Fortunately, the loudspeakers separated my friendly fireman and me. (Saved by the bell, so to speak.) The staff was now being requested to leave the Store as well. But not Paris. To help the police with their inquiries. Merry Xmas.

At the end of the toy counter I grabbed a multi-coloured ball and shoved it into my pocket. One of those translucent things which bounce about forever. I had presents to buy, too. At the next counter,

I stuffed it into some starry wrapping paper. I left my work suit in the changing rooms and went out. Outside, a closely packed crowd was waiting for the entire Store to go up in smoke. The icy temperature made me realize that I'd been sweltering. Since the crowd was outside, maybe it had left me the métro.

It was inside the métro as well.

Chapter 3

I HAVE A three-yearly renewable lease on 78, rue de la Folie-Régnault, near Père-Lachaise cemetery. As I opened the door, the phone was ringing its heart out. And whenever someone calls me up, I always come running.

"Are you all right, Ben?"

It was my sister Louna.

"What do you mean, 'all right'?"

"The bomb in the Store . . ."

"Everyone else was blown to smithereens. I'm the sole survivor."

She had a giggle. She fell silent. Then she said:

"Talking about surviving, I've made a decision."

"What sort?"

"The bombshell sort. It's about my little squatter. I'm going to evict him, Ben. Go for an abortion. Laurent's the one I want to keep."

Silence again. I could hear she was crying. But distantly. She was trying to hide that from me.

"Listen, Louna . . ."

Listen to what? It was a classic set-up. She was the nice nurse and he the handsome doctor. It was love at first sight, followed up by the decision to stare into the whites of each other's eyes until death do them part, just him and her, and no-one else. But as the years went by, the desire for a third person started taking over. The feminine craving for duplication: life.

"Listen, Louna . . ."

I could hear she was listening, but I didn't say anything. So she wound up by saying:

"I'm listening."

And then I started off. I told her that she ought to hang onto her little squatter. She'd evicted the previous ones because she hadn't loved their daddies, so she wasn't going to evict this one because she loved the daddy too much! Really, now, Louna, stop playing silly buggers! ("Stop playing silly buggers yourself," I could hear a familiar voice whisper from somewhere within. "You'll be giving her the 'right to life' angle next!") But I'd started, so I was going to finish:

"Anyway, things will never be the same again. You'll end up holding it against Laurent, I just know you will. And then it won't be a pair of ovaries being dangled under the abortionist's nose, it'll be more like a long lingering case of consumption, if you see what I mean."

She cried, she laughed, she cried again. For half an hour!

I'd only just hung up, feeling all in, when it rang again.

"Hello, number one son, is everything all right?"

It was mum.

"Fine, mum, just fine."

"A bomb at the Store! Just imagine it. Nothing like that would ever have happened in our place!"

What she meant was in the lovely little hardware shop downstairs, where I spent my childhood not learning DIY and which we'd finally turned into a flat for the kids. But she was forgetting about Morel, the grocer over the road, and his iron grill which got blown away by a lump of jelly one morning in June 1962. She was forgetting about the visit of two men in double-breasted jackets who told her to pick her clientele carefully. She was sweet, was mum. She forgot all about wars.

"How are the kids?"

"The kids are fine. They're downstairs."

"What are you doing for Xmas?"

"The five of us are spending it here."

"Robert's taking me to Châlons."

(Châlons-sur-Marne? Poor old mum.) I said:

"Good old Robert!"

She chuckled.

"You're a good boy, number one son."

(Yes, what a good boy am I . . .)

"Your other children aren't so bad either, mother mine."

"That's thanks to you, Benjamin, you've always been a good boy."

(After the chuckle, the sob.)

"What with me abandoning you . . ."

(What a bad mother is she . . .)

"You're not abandoning us, mum, you're just having a rest. You're resting!"

"What sort of a mother am I, Ben, can you tell me that? What sort of a mother am I . . . ?"

As I'd already timed exactly how long she was going to need to answer her own questions, I gently laid the receiver on my eiderdown and went into the kitchen to make myself a frothy cup of Turkish coffee. When I got back to the bedroom, the phone was still trying to unravel my mother's identity . . .

". . . it was the first time I ran away from home, Ben, I was three years old . . ."

When I'd drunk my coffee, I turned the cup over onto the saucer. Thérèse could have read the futures of the entire neighbourhood in the dense layer of grounds that formed on it.

". . . but that one was much later, I was about eight or nine years old, I think . . . Ben, are you listening to me?"

Just then, the intercom crackled into life.

"I am listening to you, mum, but I'm going to have to leave you. The kids are intercomming me! Go on, you have a well-earned rest and, don't forget, good old Robert!"

I hung up and answered. Thérèse's dry voice flayed my eardrums:

"Ben, Jeremy's pissing me off. He won't do his homework!"

"Watch your language, Thérèse. Don't start talking like your brother."

Sure enough, it was then her brother's voice which broke in:

"It's her who's fucking me off! The silly bitch can't explain anything!"

"Watch your tongue, Jeremy. Don't start talking like your sister. Put me though to Clara, will you?"

"Benjamin?"

It was Clara's warm voice. Made of the finest green felt, stretched out tight, with each and every word rolling across it with the silent inevitability of a gleaming white cue ball.

"Clara? How's Half Pint?"

"His temperature's gone down. But I still asked Laurent to call by again. He says he should stay at home wrapped up warm for another couple of days."

"Has he drawn any more Xmas Ogres?"

"A dozen of them. But they're a lot less red. I've taken photographs of them. And, Ben, I've made us a gratin Dauphinois for this evening. It'll be ready in an hour's time."

"I'll be there. Hand me over to Half Pint."

And Half Pint's half pint voice crackled across:

"Yes, Ben?"

"Nothing. I just wanted to tell you that Theo's given you another photo for your album and that, this evening, I'm going to tell you a new story."

"A story about ogres?"

"A story about bombs."

"Oh yes? That's great then . . ."

"Now I'm going to have an hour's kip. If you see anyone go near the intercom, kill them."

"OK, Ben."

I hung up and flopped down onto my bed, asleep before I'd even landed.

An hour later, what woke me up was a huge dog. He hit me with a flank attack. Under the force of impact, I rolled down to the end of the bed and wound up stuck against the wall. He took advantage of the situation by pinning me down and starting to give me the wash I hadn't had time to have that morning. But he stank like a public waste tip. His tongue smelt like a cross between a rotten fish, tiger sperm and essence of Paris's dog life.

I said:

"Presie?"

He leapt backwards, slumped down onto his unmentionable behind and, with his tongue dangling, stared at me with his head to one side. I dipped my hand into my jacket pocket and produced the little gift-wrapped ball, which I presented to him and declared:

"For Julius. Merry Xmas!"

Downstairs in the ex-hardware shop, the nutmeg odour of gratin Dauphinois lingered for ages in the air after I'd drawn the kids into the heart of my tale. Above their pyjamas, their eyes were agog, while their feet dangled in mid-air between the bunk beds. I'd reached the moment when Lehmann forced his way through to the runaway roller coaster. He shoved the crowds aside with mighty blows from the metal arm I'd specially invented for him.

"How did he lose his real arm?" Jeremy asked at once.

"In Indochina, on the 317th kilometre of the Dalat road, during an ambush. His men loved him so much that they all legged it and abandoned him there, him and his arm, which had already parted company."

"So how did he make it back?"

"His company captain came and fetched him all on his own, three days later."

"Three days later! So what did he have to eat during those three days?" Half Pint asked.

"His arm!"

A crafty reply, which satisfied them all: Half Pint had had his ogre story, Jeremy his war story and Clara her touch of humour; as for Thérèse, sitting as stiff as a court usher behind her desk, she was as usual taking my whole story down in shorthand, asides included.

It was excellent training for her secretarial school. During two years of nightly practice, she'd already copied out *The Brothers Karamazov*, *Moby Dick, Fantasia in Hickland, Gosta Boerling, Asphalt Jungle*, plus a couple of products of my own mental stockroom.

So I kept on narrating, till the fluttering of eyelids showed that the lights were going out. As I closed the door behind me, the Xmas tree sparkled in the darkness. I'd done a pretty good job. The idea of diving onto their presents hadn't even occurred to them. Only to Julius, who'd just spent the last two hours trying hard to open his parcel without ripping the paper.

Chapter 4

WHAT HAPPENED NEXT was announced by a ring of the door bell, the following day, December 25, at eight o'clock in the morning. I was about to yell out: "Come in, it's open," but a bad memory held me back. That was how Julius and I ended up having a white wooden coffin delivered to us the previous week, right there in the middle of the corridor, flanked by three constipated-looking delivery men. The most pasty-faced one of them simply said:

"It's for the corpse."

Julius ran off to hide under the bed and I, with my hair all over the place and my eyes glazed, just pointed apologetically at my pyjamas.

"Come back in fifty years' time. I'm afraid I'm not ready yet."

So, anyway, someone was ringing the bell. I dragged myself as far as the door, with Julius in tow, who's always into making new acquaintances. A bull-necked hunk, done up in a flying jacket complete with fur collar, stood there in front of me like an Irish paratrooper who'd just been dropped into German-occupied France.

"Trainee Inspector Caregga."

A pig's ear who'd been turned into a silk purse. No sooner had he squeezed his immense bulk into the flat, than his buttocks got a thorough visiting from Julius's snout. The copper then promptly sat himself down, but without thumping my dog. Which is perhaps in part why I suggested:

"Coffee?"

"If you're having one . . ."

I headed off for the kitchen. He asked me:

"You never lock your front door?"

"Never."

The phrase "my dog's sexual liberation would not permit it" crossed my mind, but remained unspoken.

"I have one or two questions to ask you. Routine stuff."

It was just what I'd been expecting. A nice little wake-up call for the Store's cherished employees. Ten or twelve shop stewards and the same number of mavericks being the first to receive the boys in blue. A Xmas present from the management to their little favourites.

"Are you married?" The sugared water was gurgling in the copper coffee-pot.

"No."

I tipped in three spoonfuls of ground Turkish coffee and stirred gently until it became as smooth as Clara's voice.

"Who do the kids downstairs belong to?"

Then I placed the entire preparation on the gas ring to heat it all through, while being very careful not to let the coffee boil.

"They're my mother's kids, my half-siblings."

When his pencil'd finished colouring in his little notepad, Inspector Caregga fired off the next question:

"And the fathers?"

"Gone with the wind."

I glanced through the kitchen door. Caregga was carefully noting down the fact that my poor mother's men friends went with the wind. Then, armed with the coffee-pot and cups, I made my entrance. I poured out the rich liquid. I stopped the Inspector's hand as it stretched out.

"Wait a bit. You have to let the grounds settle before drinking."

He let them settle.

Sitting at his feet, Julius was looking at him passionately.

"What do you do exactly at the Store?"

"I get bollocked."

No reaction. He wrote it down.

"Any previous employment?"

Goodness me, the list was going to be quite a long one: warehouse man, barman, taxi driver, art teacher in a convent school, soap market-researcher, a few others I'd probably forgotten, then Quality Controller at the Store, my latest job.

"Since when?"

"Four months."

"You like it?"

"It's just the same as everything else. Far too highly paid for what I do, but not high enough considering the boredom factor."

(Let's try and up the tone of the conversation a little, for Christ's sake!)

He wrote it down.

"You didn't notice anything unusual yesterday?"

"Yes. A bomb went off."

That finally did make him lift his head. But it was just to make his question clearer in the same unflappable tone:

"No, I mean *before* the explosion."

"Nothing."

"Apparently you were called in three times to the Customer Complaints Office."

Here we go. I told him all about the gas cooker, the Hoover and the fire-raising fridge.

He rummaged through an inside pocket, then laid out a plan of the Store in front of me.

"Where is the Customer Complaints Office?"

I pointed it out to him.

"So you went in front of the toy counter at least three times?"

What a brainy bugger!

"Yes, I did."

"Did you stop there?"

"For about ten seconds the third time round."

"Notice anything unusual?"

"Apart from the fact that I was being held at gun point by an AMX 30 tank, not a thing."

He noted that down in silence, put the top back on his pen, knocked back his coffee in one, grounds included, got up and said:

"That will be all for now. Don't leave Paris. We might have some more questions to ask you. Thanks for the coffee. Goodbye."

I realized then that it wasn't only in films that people stand gaping for ages at a door that's just closed. Julius and I were both under the spell of Inspector Caregga's open-hearted charm. That lad had quite a future before him in the Laughing Squad. But he had given me an idea for the tale I was going to spin the kids that evening. It would be the same thing, but with sparkling, incredibly witty repartee, which would be evenly distributed in a mixture of hatred, mistrust and admiration, plus there would be two coppers, that terrible twosome I'd invented and which the kids knew well: a small hairy one, as twisted and as ugly as a hyena, and a big bald one, hairless except for his sideburns – "which landed like exclamation marks onto his powerful jaws."

"Harry Hyena and Sid Burns!" Half Pint would yell out.

"Harry Hyena by name and Harry Hyena by nature," Jeremy would declare.

"Sid Burns by name and Sid Burns by gnasher," Half Pint would declare.

"Meaner than Phil Coffin and more bent than the Bouncing Czech."

"Are they friends?" Clara would ask.

"They've been together now for fifteen years," I would reply. "And have saved each other's lives more often than you've had hot dinners."

"What sort of motor do they drive?" Jeremy would ask, because he loved the answer.

"A pink six-cylinder Peugeot 504 convertible, as lethal as a pike."

"And their star signs?" Thérèse would ask.

"Taurus, both of them."

* * *

When I got back to the children after Caregga's departure, the Xmas tree was ablaze with light. Jeremy and Half Pint were squawking like gulls over a sea of wrapping paper. Thérèse, with a professional frown, was copying out last night's tale onto a spanking new daisy-wheel typewriter. Louna, who had dropped in, was watching over this family tableau with a tear in her eye and her feet splayed out, like she was already six months pregnant. I noted Laurent's absence. Clara drifted over towards me in a knitted dress, which gave her a mature vibrant woman's body. She was holding the old Leica camera which she'd been silently coveting for years and which I'd finally surrendered to her photographic passion. The dress had been chosen by Theo. In that field, always ask the advice of a man that prefers men. (This might be a false impression of mine.)

"Here, Benjamin, this is for you."

What Clara handed me came in a beautifully wrapped parcel. It was inside a cardboard box, then inside some silky paper. It was a pair of granddad slippers, with whipped cream piping. It was exactly what I wanted. That's Xmas for you.

Chapter 5

ON BOXING DAY, it was back to work. Just like every day, Julius went with me as far as Père-Lachaise métro station, then sloped off to kerbcrawl Belleville while I was off bringing home the Pedigree Chum. His brand new ball had been stuck between his dribbling jaws since the evening of the day before yesterday.

In the paper I'd just bought, they dwelt at length on "the inhuman bombing of the Store". Since just one casualty wasn't enough for them, a journalist described in his piece *what might have happened* if there'd been ten of them! (Wake yourself up if you really want a nightmare . . .)Then the hack got round to giving us a short biography of the deceased. He'd been an honest garage mechanic from Courbevoie, aged sixty-two, dearly regretted by one and all in his neighbourhood and who had been, "thanks be to God", single and childless. No, I wasn't seeing things. I really had just read "thanks be to God single and childless". I took a look around. The fact that the Lord of Randomness, thanks be to him, blew away single people first didn't seem to unduly bother the little group of family people in the underground. This put me in such a good mood, that I got off at République with the intention of walking the rest of the way. It was a dark winter's morning, icy cold, slithery and traffic jammed. Paris was a puddle blotched with the yellow light of headlamps.

I'd been afraid of arriving late, but the Store was even later than I was. With its iron shutters drawn down over its huge windows it looked like a steam ship in a dry dock. Vapour was rising from its underground boiler room and vanishing in flurries into the morning mist. Here and there, glimpses of light coming from the inside revealed that its heart was still beating. There was life in it yet. So in I went, and was at once bathed in light. It was the same shock every time. The darker and more sinister it was on the outside, the brighter it shone on the inside. All that light beaming down in a silent cascade from the Store's upper reaches, rebounding off the mirrors, the copper plating, the panes of glass, the fake crystal, flowing away down the aisles, sprinkling your soul – all that brightness didn't light up the world, it reinvented it.

That's what I was daydreaming about while a nimble-fingered copper frisked me from head to toe, finally came to the conclusion that I wasn't a walking atomic bomb and let me in.

I wasn't the first one there. Most of the staff was already mustered in the aisles of the ground floor. They were all staring up into space. Most of them were women. Their eyes were sparkling with a suspect gleam, like they were waiting for the Holy Ghost to come down on them. High up there on his captain's bridge, Sainclair was purring into a microphone. He was paying homage to "the perfect bearing of the staff" during the recent "occurrence". He gave all of the management's best wishes to Chantredon – the bloke who'd taken a dive through a cosmetic display case and who was now licking his wounds in hospital. He apologized to all those who had received visits from the police yesterday. The entire staff, "management included", would be going through the same thing, but the sole and unique objective was "to help the police as much as possible with their inquiries and so hasten them on towards a happy conclusion".

As far as Sainclair himself was concerned he couldn't believe for a moment that the bomb had been planted by one of his "fellow members of staff". For we were not his "employees", but his "fellow members of staff", just as he'd once solemnly declared during a Trade Union meeting with the management. A thousand pardons to his "fellow members of staff" for the swift once-over on their way in. He, too, had agreed to be searched and so would each and every customer until the police's investigations were over.

I stared up at Sainclair. He was very young. He was very handsome. He was on the fast lane. His authority was lightly carried. He was fresh out from some up-market business school where the first thing they teach you is how to modulate your voice and pick your clothes. The rest follows on naturally. He spoke almost tenderly and, under his blond fringe, a gentle stare tinged with sadness filtered across. Sainclair felt bad for the Store. The fellow members of staff at either side of him, the personnel manager, the floor managers, the top-class turnkeys, all looked more the part. They were lined up along the gilded first-floor handrail. Their faces were fit for the occasion. Listen attentively, and you could hear medals springing out onto their responsible chests. The idea made me laugh. So I laughed. The bloke in front of me turned round. It was Lecyfre, the hard-line commie shop steward, in flesh and bloody-mindedness.

"Leave it out, Malaussène. Just shut your nasty little gob."

I glanced back around the ecstatic crowd, then at the sleek nape of Lecyfre's neck, then once more at the official platform. Sainclair had a gift, there was no doubt about it. He'd twigged something that I was never going to fathom.

I let the mass go on without me and went off to the changing rooms. I opened my locker and got out my work suit. It wasn't mine. It had been lent to me by my employers. Neither too dated, nor too with it. Just a nice little hint of greyness, aging and excessive honesty. The suit of a man who'd like to be able to buy himself a new one. I held it out at arm's length, as if I was looking at it for the first time. A mocking voice woke me from my daydream:

"Are you on the sniff, Ben? Want to borrow one of mine?"

It was Theo, who'd togged himself up in Cerutti that morning. He changed clothes so often for his photo booth sessions that his locker was chock full of them and they'd even started colonizing my one as well. Our keys were common property. Every morning I extracted my work suit from his collection of Hollywood wop designer rags.

"No kidding. If you fancy one, just help yourself!"

I waved away his offer.

"No thanks, Theo. I was just wondering from the jolliness of my uniform whether I was really the man for the job."

He burst out laughing.

"That's exactly what I ask myself every morning in front of my wardrobe. I say to myself that I was made to be straight, and here I am, gay."

Upon which, the two of us headed down into the basement, the DIY kingdom, Theo's empire. Every morning, he turned up a good half an hour before his sales staff. He paced up and down the empty aisles, like Napoleon in front of his assembled troops before the massacre. The slightest nut missing from the array was spotted at once, the smallest hint of confusion in the display cases cut him to the quick.

"Don't my little oldsters make a right fucking mess of the place!"

He sighed. He put it all back as it should be. He could have tidied the entire basement blindfolded. It was his manor. When the two of us were alone there, it was plunged into a silence from before the creation of the world.

"Did Clara like her dress?"

"Beautiful dress, beautiful girl, Theo."

We spoke in whispers. He found an electric bell in a bin full of armchair casters.

"You see, what snaps first in my oldsters is their memory. They pick up one thing, then drop it any old where so as to pick up the next thing. They're as grabbing and acquisitive as toddlers . . ."

The reign of Theo's little oldsters dated back to the days when he'd been a simple tool salesman. He'd been so nice to all the neighbourhood leftovers that more and more of them had come along to work for days on end on his workbenches.

"I come from off the street. I know what it's like. So I don't want to leave them there. They might get led astray."

That was his answer whenever someone complained about this invasion of centenarians.

"When here, they feel like they're rebuilding their world, and it doesn't cost us a penny."

The higher Theo climbed up the ladder, the more numerous the little oldsters became. They came from the farthest-flung hospices. And, since Sainclair had crowned him the DIY Emperor (not only could he rebuild Paris with whatever was to hand, but he could sell a lawnmower to someone who was refitting his bathroom), the entirety of the basement was Theo's oldsters' playground.

"It's a foretaste of heaven for them."

"Where did you unearth all those grey smocks from?"

"From the closing down sale of an orphanage near where I live. At least with those things on, I can keep tabs on them all."

At noon, in the small restaurant where we went to avoid the staff canteen, Theo had an attack of the giggles.

"Do you know what?"

"No, what?"

"Lehmann's putting it about that I'm a gerontophile. Like a paedophile, only for pensioners, get me?"

(Good old Lehmann . . .)

"Talking about paedophilia, give this to Half Pint for his album, will you?"

It was another little snap. A burgundy suit of velvet silk with a mimosa in the buttonhole. On the back, the following rubric, which Half Pint would copy out in his best round hand:

"This is Theo when he goes boating on the Seine."

What that meant was anyone's guess. But Theo knew. And Theo's countless friends knew as well, whenever they found these photographic messages pinned up on his front door when he was out. So what about Half Pint? Should I outlaw this collection? I knew that kiddies weren't Theo's department, but all the same . . .

Chapter 6

AT THE BEGINNING of the afternoon, a couple of complaints had already dropped into my in-tray. Including a serious cock-up in the bedding department. Lehmann had me called up. I headed off past the toy counter. There wasn't a trace of the blast left. The counter hadn't been repaired, but replaced, during the night, by a new and completely identical one. It was a weird impression, just as though there'd never been any explosion and I'd been the victim of a mass hallucination. As though someone was trying to chop a lump out of my memory. Those were the depressing thoughts that were running through my mind while the escalator plunged the toy counter into the seething depths of the Store.

The character who was doing the moaning in Lehmann's office had a pair of shoulders so broad that they blocked the entire glass door. A back fit to eclipse the sun. Which meant that I couldn't see Lehmann's face. To judge by the twitching muscles under the customer's jacket and the throbbing vein in his bright red neck, old Lehmann was certainly up shit creek. What he'd got standing in front of him was not exactly the jolly green giant. It was someone of the self-confident sort, who didn't raise its voice. The worst of the lot. He hadn't walked right into the office. He'd just closed the door behind him and started muttering out his grievances with his finger pointing at Lehmann. I gave the door three discreet knocks. Barely a tap, tap, tap.

"Come in!"

Oh dear! The panic in Lehmann's voice! The colossus opened the door himself, without turning round. I slipped in between his arm and the door frame with all the craven suppleness of a beaten dog.

"Three days in hospital and a fortnight off work. I'm going to have your Quality Controller's guts for garters."

That was the customer speaking. In a neutral voice, just as I'd feared, full of deadly certainty. He wasn't there to complain, nor to argue, nor even to demand anything – he'd quite simply come to get his due and no messing. You only had to glance at him to see that that was the way he always went about things. And you only had to glance at him again to see that this had not allowed him to clamber very far up the social ladder. His heart must have got in his way somehow. But Lehmann didn't sniff characters out like that. He was used to doing the punching and so was only frightened of one thing: getting punched back. And seen from that angle, our man certainly looked impressive.

I put enough terror into my eyes for Lehmann finally to pluck up the courage to bring me into the conversation. The long and short of it was that our Mr So-and-So, a professional deep-sea diver (why tell me that? to guarantee the muscle?), had ordered a double bed the previous week from our solid wood furniture department.

"And solid wood's your sector, isn't it, Malaussène?"

My pate nodded timidly.

"So, he ordered a hand-sawn walnut double bed, reference number T.P.885, from your department, Monsieur Malaussène, and the two legs at the head of this bed snapped during the first night."

A pause. I glanced at the deep-sea diver, whose lower jaw was massacring a scrap of chewing gum. Then I glanced at Lehmann, who was looking rather relieved at having passed me the parcel.

"The guarantee . . ." said I.

"The guarantee will be respected, but your responsibility goes further than that, otherwise I wouldn't have called you in here."

I took a good long look at my shoes.

"There was someone else in that bed."

Even when shitting himself, Lehmann couldn't resist this sort of amusement.

"A young lady, if you see what I mean . . ."

But the rest evaporated under the blow torch from the colossus's eyes. And he was the one who rounded off:

"A collarbone and two ribs. My fiancée. In hospital."

"Oooh!"

My scream was a genuine one. A scream of pain. Which made them both jump.

"Oooh!"

Just like I'd been punched in the guts. Then, by digging my elbow into my rib cage, just below my nipple, I went as white as the sheets on that fatal bed. Hercules took a step forwards and even put his hands out to catch me in case I passed out.

"I did that?"

My voice was strangled and wan. Staggering, I leant on Lehmann's desk.

"I did that?"

The thought of that heap of muscle diving down from its spring board onto Louna or Clara and smashing every bone in their bodies was enough to have real tears start pouring. And it was a sodden, streaked face which asked him:

"What is her name?"

The rest was child's play. Sincerely moved by my emotional state, Mr Atlas suddenly unwound. Quite a sight. His heart almost popped out onto his sleeve. Lehmann grabbed the chance to lay straight into me. Sobbing, I said I'd resign. Sneering, he said that that would be too easy. I started to beg, claiming that the Store could hardly have expected any better from such a useless worm as me.

"Uselessness has to be paid for, Malaussène! Just like everything else. *Even more* than everything else!"

And he threatened to make me pay so dearly for my uselessness that our massive customer suddenly strode across the office and slammed his two fists down onto Lehmann's desk.

"Do you get your kicks out of tormenting lads like this?"

The "lad" in question was my good self. So there I was, under the Lord High Muscleman's protection. Lehmann was wishing he had a deeper desk chair. Our man started getting things off his chest. Already, when still at school, it had used to do his head in seeing big bullies picking on smaller kids.

"So you listen to me now, you creep."

The "creep" was Lehmann, who'd gone off white. Like a pile of ash waiting to be swept up. What he had to listen to was straightforward enough. Firstly, our man was withdrawing his complaint. Secondly, he'd be back in person to check I still had my job. Thirdly, if I wasn't there any more, if Lehmann'd had me fired . . .

"I'll snap you in two, like this!"

"This" was Lehmann's lovely ebony ruler, a souvenir from colonial days, which had just cracked between my saviour's fingers.

Lehmann was not really himself again until the escalator had gobbled up every last cubic inch of our colossus. Then finally he slapped his thigh and started cackling like a hyena. I didn't share his amusement. Not that time. I'd followed our retreating muscleman all the way out ("Don't let those shit-heads get you, my lad, get them first!" is what he'd told me as we parted) and once again I started talking to myself as if I was someone else. Mr Universe thought he was going to attack the Store, an Empire or, at the very least, the Quality Control Department, some powerful anonymous institution, and so had armed himself accordingly. Bayard in person, ready to bring a whole garrison down to its knees single-handed. Then, lo and behold, he comes up against one of the eternal losers (you, Malaussène!), who looks like he's about to drop dead and the poor bugger melts, just like he'd always melted, from his excess human warmth. When my diver had turned on his heels, I glanced down at his shoes and thought: "I hope your flippers are in better nick."

Then it was my turn to open the door.

"I've had enough for one day, Lehmann. I'm going home. Theo can replace me if necessary."

Lehmann's laughter stuck in his throat.

"That isn't what the little poofter's paid for!"
"No-one should be paid for doing this."
He made his smile as scornful as possible before replying:
"That's exactly my opinion, too."
(You deserved getting your metal arm, fuck-face.)

When I went back down, there was a crowd seething round the toy counter.

"It's the first time we've sold more on Boxing Day than on Xmas Eve!"

This remark came from my little squirrel-faced redhead. She was talking to a friend of hers, a sort of weasel, who was busy wrapping up a Boeing 747. The friend nodded. Her long fingers slid with incredible speed over a sheet of dark blue paper, dotted with pink stars, which immediately turned itself into a parcel. Beside the gift-wrapper, a robotized King Kong was going through its paces on a demonstration stand. It was a large, thick-set, hairy ape which looked too genuine to be true. It was walking on the spot. In its arms, it was carrying a half-naked doll, which looked like a sleeping Clara. It walked on but didn't get anywhere. From time to time, its head glanced backwards. Its red eyes and gaping mouth sent out bolts of lightning. There was a real feeling of menace in the opaque blackness of its fur, the bloody redness of its stare and that poor little body, so white in its terrible arms. (Jesus, it was true, this job really was starting to do my head in . . . and it was true that that doll really did look like my Clara . . .)

Chapter 7

When I got back home, that big black ape was still trotting through my brains. And when the phone rang, it was as much as I could do to say "hello".

"Ben?"

It was Louna.

"Ben, I'm going to evict my little squatter."

Oh no! I was in no mood for going through all that again. Not that evening.

I answered in my best nasty voice:

"What do you expect me to do about it? Become a bailiff?"

She hung up.

When I too hung up, the first thing that met my gaze was Julius the dog's grinning gob in the door frame. He hadn't dropped his ball for a single second all day. I gave him a filthy look and said:

"No, not this evening!"

He slunk straight off to his mat. And I crashed out. An hour later, I awoke and picked up the intercom.

"Clara? I need a breath of fresh air. I'll see you all after dinner."

"OK, Ben. Your Leica takes great photos. I'll show you some."

Julius was still flat out. He gawped at me with a pained, questioning look. This other master was a problem for him. Luckily enough, he didn't see him that often.

I asked:

"Fancy a walk?"

He leapt up onto his paws. He was always pleased to go out and always pleased to come home, was Julius. That's a dog for you.

The Store was not the only thing going up in smoke. Belleville was too. With all those house-fronts missing along its pavements, the boulevard looked like a grin with half its teeth knocked out. With his nose hoovering the ground, Julius was dragging his paws, his tail wagging like mad. Suddenly he squatted down in order to raise up a superb monument to canine olfaction right there in the central pathway. Then he advanced ten yards, with his baggy arse held high and proud, before abruptly coming to a halt, as if he'd forgotten something important. Then he started rabidly scratching at the tarmac with his back legs. He was nowhere near his turd, nor even in line with it, but he didn't give a damn. Julius was doing his business. A dog has to do what a dog has to do. He was no department store counter, was our Julius. He had a memory. Even if he didn't know what was in it.

A hundred yards farther down the road, a muezzin's woeful voice broke through the Belleville dusk. I knew his make-shift minaret. It was a small square window, opening onto a toilet or a landing, between the third and fourth floors of a dilapidated building. I allowed myself to be transported for a moment by the wailing of that priest from over the waters. He was bawling out a sura which had to be something about hollyhocks shooting up their sacred stalks through the Prophet's bone orchard. It was redolent of an almost unbearable sense of exile. For the first time, the image of that splattered corpse in the Store flashed through my mind. Then I thought of Louna and called myself a bastard, before that Courbevoie mechanic's guts returned. I just had the time to lean back against a tree and so avoided a second honk. I counted the steps as I crossed the road and went into the Koutoubia.

Julius dived straight into the kitchen to find Hadouch. The muezzin's voice was drowned out by the clicking of dominoes and jawing. The room was heavy with smoke and most of the customers were sitting with glasses of pastis in front of them. I thought how that Muslim brother at the window was going to have his work cut out for him if he was going to bring this lot back to the purity of Islam!

As soon as he spotted me, old Amar flashed me his broadest grin. The whiteness of his hair always astonished me. He went round the end of his bar and took me in his arms.

"How are you, my son, how are you?"

"Fine thanks."

"And how is your mother?"

"Fine too. She's resting. In Châlons."

"And how are the children?"

"Fine."

"You didn't bring them with you?"

"They're doing their homework."

"And how is your own work going?"

"Like a bomb!"

He sat me down on a chair, spread out a paper tablecloth in the twinkling of an eye, leant down in front of me on his stretched-out arms and smiled. I asked him:

"What about you, Amar, how are you?"

"I'm fine, thank you for asking."

"And how are the children?"

"They're fine, thank you for asking."

"And what about your wife? How's Yasmina?"

"She's fine, thanks be to God."

"When are you going to get the next one on the way?"

"I'm going back to Algiers next week to start off the last one."

We chuckled. Yasmina had quite often been a surrogate mum for me when I was little and my own mum was occupied elsewhere.

Amar went to look after his customers. Hadouch plopped down a couscous in front of me, which I was going to have to gulp through to the bitter end, if I didn't want to offend both the Prophet and his faithful all in the same evening.

Noticing my lack of appetite, Amar sat down in front of me.

"Things aren't that fine, are they?"

"No, they aren't."

"Shall I take you to Algiers with me?"

Whyever not? For a couple of seconds, I let the idea trace a shining path of pleasure through my brains. Amar pressed the point:

"Well? Hadouch could look after the dog and the children."

But trainee Inspector Caregga's flat face brought my thoughts back onto the straight and narrow.

"Sorry, Amar. I can't."

"Why not?"

"Because of work."

He stared incredulously at me, but told himself that one man's meat is another man's burden, got to his feet and slapped me on the shoulder.

"I'll get you some tea."

Umm Kulthum's voice sprang out from the jukebox. The massive crowd at her burial marched across the screen. I let the song fade away then, with Julius at my heels, left the place. Hadouch's laughter trickled after us for a moment:

"Next time, I'm not going to give your pooch his dinner, I'm going to give him a bath!"

I told the children about the cautious beginnings of the police inquiries, with Harry Hyena and Sid Burns sticking their noses deep into the private lives of Sainclair's "fellow members of staff", the gang of ghosts replacing the toy counter during the night, the heroism of the Store which went on selling as though nothing had happened. (A bunch of real troopers!) All around us, Clara's photos were drying on clothes lines. (How many hours' exam revision were being sacrificed to her hobby?) There were snaps of Half Pint's Xmas Ogres. Others illustrated the vanishing of Belleville and the upsurging of those smooth aquariums which would constitute the *belle ville* of the future. And then a photo of mum when she was young – from around the time I was born. With that yearning for the wild blue yonder already glittering in her eye.

"Did you have a negative?"

"No, I made a print of it."

"We'll frame her," Jeremy declared. "That way, she won't be able to leg it again."

Thérèse indiscriminately took the lot down in shorthand, as though it was all part of one big novel. Then, all of a sudden, she fixed her anorexic nun's stare on me:

"Ben?"

"Thérèse?"

"The casualty, that Courbevoie mechanic . . ."

"What about him?"

"I drew up his birth chart. He was destined to die like that."

Clara glanced across rapidly at me. I checked that Half Pint was asleep and gave Jeremy one of my looks which dried up his usual backchat. That out of the way, I made my handsome face look as interested as I could manage.

"Go on, we're all ears."

"He was born on January 21, 1919, Ben, they said so in his obituary. On that very day, Mars was in conjunction with Uranus at 325°, and both of them were in opposition to Saturn at 146°."

"With whose anus?"

"Shut up, Jeremy."

"Mars, the planet of action, in conjunction with Uranus, for violent disorder, in opposition to Saturn indicates an evil, creative personality."

"So Mars bars the way?"

"Jeremy, shut up."

"Mars and Uranus in the eighth house announce a violent death, which was actually to come to pass when Mars crossed over a radical moon, and this was precisely the case on December 24!"

"So Uranus was mooning?"

"Jeremy . . ."

Chapter 8

THERE WAS NO bomb the next day. And none the day after. Nor during the following days. My workmates slowly started to calm down again. Soon no-one was talking about it any more. It was nothing but a distant memory. The Store was at cruising speed once again. It sailed well clear of any explosive risks. Lehmann played at being Mr Midshipman Easy even more eagerly than ever. Theo's little oldsters felt like empire builders. Theo himself added to Half Pint's album every day. The coppers continued to frisk the staff and the customers, who lifted high their arms with smiles on their faces. Sainclair had lost his eight hundred fellow members of staff and regained eight hundred employees. Lecyfre relayed the C.G.T. trade union pronouncements, just as Lehmann did for the management. I got well and truly bollocked. Lost in my vacant imagination, Harry Hyena and Sid Burns were starting to run out of steam. The kids threatened to replace me with a telly if I didn't come up with something. Louna had stopped phoning me. Everything went back to normal. Until February 2.

She was a real beauty. Like a lioness. Her red hair tumbled down in dense waves over her broad, visibly muscular shoulders. She had Italian hips which swayed gracefully. She was no longer a youngster. She'd reached the age of pleasant plenitude. The top of her skirt, squeezed against her buttocks, made visible a skimpy panty line. As I had nothing else to do but wait for Miss Hamilton's call, I decided to cruise after my vision of beauty. Here and there she fingered articles on the shelves. Her half-naked arms were ringed with

Oriental-looking jewellery. She had long, tanned, supple fingers which sprang out before seizing an object. I followed her with the ease of the dog-fish I had now become in the troubled waters of the Store. I played at losing her so that I'd have the pleasure of finding her at the crossing of two aisles. At these not really chance encounters, I let my adrenaline bristle up every interior hair in my body. Only one thing bothered me. I never managed to meet her eyes. Her head of hair was too ample. And too springy. As for her, she obviously didn't notice me. (My work suit made me see-through.) This carry-on continued for some time. I'd reached a state of absolute desire when what happened happened. She'd been hanging around in front of the Shetland sweater counter for a good five minutes. Suddenly, her fingers sprang out, uncurled, snaffled up an entire small pullover into the palm of her hand. The hand then dived into her bag, where it was swallowed up before being spat back out again empty.

I saw her. But, from the other side of the counter, Cazeneuve the store detective had seen her too. Luckily I was closer to her than he was. While he was rounding the counter and starting to bare his teeth, I took the two steps forwards which separated me from my lovely shoplifter. While spinning her round to face me, I shoved my hand into her bag, pulled out the sweater and stuck it up against her shoulders, like I was making her try it on. Meanwhile, with a thoughtful look, I murmured from between my teeth:

"Don't play silly buggers, now, the departmental dick is right behind you."

Not only did she react fast enough so as not to struggle, she even replied in a beautiful husky voice:

"It's really me, don't you think so?"

Taken aback, all I could do was to blurt out:

"It goes perfectly with your eyes, Aunt Julia, but not with your hair."

In fact, I only had eyes for her eyes. They were two almonds, sprinkled with gold dust, edged by lashes which were almost tickling my nose. Behind these beauties, another pair of eyes was looking daggers at me. Cazeneuve's peepers. I casually dropped the sweater onto the counter, picked out another one and, holding my head back with a connoisseur's expression on my face, I handed it to the girl. Cazeneuve had now recovered his wits and butted in. He didn't beat about the bush:

"Leave it out, Malaussène, I saw this bird nick that sweater."

"*This bird*, Cazeneuve? Is that any way for a nice boy like you to talk about our clientele?"

I announced this in a far-off voice, like I was miles away. The second sweater (that's it! I should go into the rag trade) suited my lioness to perfection. I said:

"This one was made for you, Aunt Julia."

I was not the only person admiring my "Aunt Julia". A number of customers were holding their breath. Including a nice-looking old couple with snow-white hair, a green shopping bag, and who were staring passionately at me.

"Please, Malaussène, don't obstruct me in my duty."

Cazeneuve's teeth were grating. Meanwhile, just near us, one of Theo's little oldsters was pocketing a vibrator.

"I'm not obstructing you in your duty, I'm just stopping you enjoying it too much."

"You put that Shetland sweater in your bag, young lady, I saw you!"

The girl hung onto my eyes like they were a lifebuoy. Her face was wide, her cheekbones high, her lips moist.

"And do I ask you why you're so sun-tanned, Cazeneuve?"

Bull's-eye. Cazeneuve got his pretty terracotta mug rebaked every day, free gratis and for nothing, in the Store's sun-lamp department. I added:

"Leave Aunt Julia alone, or I'll smash your face in."

That's when it happened, like it was all in slow motion, in a Store that had suddenly come to a complete standstill. Cazeneuve went white. Just behind him, the lovely old couple had turned smilingly to each other. Then, despite being at least a hundred, they started snogging away! It was a contagiously sensuous kiss. Incredibly so. Between their tightly pressed bellies, I made out the corner of a green shopping bag. Apple green.

And, as promised, Cazeneuve got his face smashed in. But not by me. By the old lady's torn-off arm. I watched the perfect curve drawn by the geyser of blood that was spurting out of her. I could clearly see the man's face, the look of disbelief under his fringe of white hair, as soft as a baby's and cut in Julius Caesar style. I could see Cazeneuve's bonce. His cheek, suddenly gone limp, relaying the shock wave to the rest of his face.

And it was only then that I heard the explosion. A brick wall being blown to smithereens inside my skull. Thrown forwards, Cazeneuve floored Aunt Julia and me.

Chapter 9

THE GOOD POINT about being at the scene of an explosion is that you don't get trampled on. Everyone flees the epicentre.

The weight of the girl lying on top of me pinned me down onto the floor. It was like she was protecting me from enemy fire. But, having taken a closer look, it turned out that she'd quite simply fainted. Cradling her head in my hand, I rolled her gently onto her side and pulled her skirt down over her legs. Cazeneuve was sitting in front of me, gawping like a toddler in front of its first sand castle. He was covered in blood and something inside him was motionlessly wondering whether it was his or someone else's. (It was the first time I'd seen him think.) A few yards behind Cazeneuve, two corpses, which were at once interlaced and blown apart, were lying in a stew of blood and guts. I got painfully to my feet. Around me, it was the panic of the aquarium at culling time. All the fish were trying to leap out onto the floor. They sprang up, flopped back, barged into one another, then suddenly changed direction as if they were escaping from some invisible landing net. The weirdest thing was that this was all going on in an underwater silence. Entire display cases collapsed, clothes dummies were being smashed to pieces under people's feet as they fled. *Without making a sound.* I was right at the bottom of a massive goldfish bowl that was running amuck. Then Aunt Julia came to as well. I could see her lips moving, but couldn't hear a thing. *Deaf.* The blast had *deafened me.* I instinctively put my fingers to my ears. No blood. That reassured me a bit. I crouched down in front of Aunt Julia and took her face in my hands.

"Nothing broken?"

My voice sounded like I was speaking to myself on the phone. The girl answered something, then went to turn round. But I stopped her. Mind you, that closely knit bloody mess didn't make me want to puke. Not this time. Apparently, you can get used to anything. The two bodies looked like they'd swapped their guts in a sort of ultimate communion. They'd merged. There wasn't a trace left of that little apple-green shopping bag. Their two bellies had been nestling it, then it had hatched. Two men in white coats took away our completely dazed Cazeneuve. Someone tapped me on the shoulder. I turned round. The fact that History always repeats itself for the worse was confirmed in the presence of the little fireman I'd seen last time, who was trying to explain what had happened to me. A pair of pink slugs were wriggling around under his thin moustache. But – thank Christ – I couldn't hear him.

I spent four long hours in hospital. They examined me inside and out. Nothing broken. I experienced a childish pleasure at letting myself be fingered. Just like when I was a kid and was being given my bath by mum or else by Yasmina, old Amar's wife. My deafness made the whole thing even more agreeable. I'd always thought that I'd be good at being deaf but lousy at being blind. Take away the world of sound, that was fine by me. Block my eyes, and I'd drop dead. But, as all good things must come to an end, the world finally managed to force its way through to my eardrums once more. I could hear the nurses and the medics chattering around me. To begin with, I couldn't understand a word, like they were speaking in the room next door. Then it got clearer. What they wanted was to keep me in for a week's observation. There could well be complications in my brainbox. A week in hospital! Just think of the kids and Julius.

"No way!"

A tall white coat topped with a horsy face leant down over me.

"Did you say something?"

"Yes, I said 'no'. I don't want to stay here. I feel fine. Really I do. I'll be off home now."

The white coat questioned an even whiter coat, stretched out over a round belly.

"We can't just let you go like that, old chap. Not until we've taken all the necessary x-rays."

I was still lying on the table. That huge stomach was speaking right in front of my nose. All those booby-trapped bellies. What if this one went off in my face as well?

"Nor can you keep me here against my will."

Outside, it had been night for some time. As I headed off towards the métro, a car crawled along the kerb until it was level with me. Then it hooted. It was a horn from the fifties. One of those ones that went "toot". I turned round. Aunt Julia, sitting inside a lemon-yellow 4CV, was waving me to come on board.

"Are you walking? Jump in. I'll give you a lift."

So I jumped into Aunt Julia's jalopy.

"Did they make you discharge yourself? Me too. It's only normal, they do have to cover themselves."

She drove her 4CV as if it was a steamship, without the slightest jolt. If you know this make of car, then you'll realize that this was quite a feat. We meandered off towards Père-Lachaise and Aunt Julia got talking. She talked, but in my mind's eye I could see that apple-green shopping bag and those two stomachs moving together. Then the terrified look on Cazeneuve's face. He was unharmed. I'd stake my own balls on that. He was just a bit concussed. The bomb had gone off in the air-tight nest formed by those two bellies. Like it was in the middle of a soft-boiled egg.

"They had hard-ons like angels!"

Angels with hard-ons? What angels? Who had a hard-on? Aunt Julia glanced at me with an indescribable look of nostalgia in her eyes. She said:

"The Sandinistas. They had hard-ons like angels. Eternal ones. They laughed as they fucked. And, when they came, it was in long hot spurts until my fires had been completely extinguished. I had experienced that just once before, in Cuba, the day after the revolution there. I was fourteen. It was two days before my father the consul was sacked. I've been back there since, but it was all over. Replaced by the erection of Socialist Realism, Stakhanovite intercourse . . ."

She went quiet for a moment. Just the time for me to get my breath back. (Was it the bomb blast that had got her going like that?) A red light went green. Aunt Julia started up again at the same time as her car:

"Now Nicaragua's buggered as well . . . with constructive pleasure."

Her face, disfigured by an expression of disgust, immediately smoothed out and her beautiful husky voice went on with its pleasant litany:

"Fortunately, there are still the Mois left, the Maoris and the Satares . . ."

I said:

"The Satares?"

"The Satares of Brazilian Amazonia!"

She enlarged:

"They have long, straight, clearly formed muscles. Their shoulders and hips don't melt under your fingers. Their pricks have a satiny smoothness which I've never encountered elsewhere. And when they penetrate you, they light up on the inside, like a superbly bronzed Gallé 1900."

And so, while Paris's winter darkness drifted past the edge of our canoe, Aunt Julia enlarged on the superb corpus of her theory. According to her, the only people who fucked correctly were revolutionaries the day after the final victory and primitive tribes. Both of them had eternity in their souls, they screwed in the present continuous, as though it was never going to stop. Everywhere else in the world we coupled in the past or future tenses, remembering or constructing, perpetuating ourselves or multiplying, but never really looking after ourselves . . .

Her voice had become incredibly convincing:

"I mean look after ourselves here and now, one looking after the other, at that very instant, after you and after me . . ."

My lights lit up on Aunt Julia. I didn't take my eyes off her for a second. Her form had become iridescent in the city lights. Then suddenly, in the gleam of a shop window full of lamps, she appeared to me in her entirety. (Mamma mia! . . .)

Chapter 10

WE LEFT THE car double parked, we legged it up the two flights of stairs like we were running for our lives, we leapt onto my bed like it was a sand dune, we tore our clothes off like they were on fire, her two breasts burst out into my face, her mouth clamped itself onto mine, my mouth discovered the vibrant kiss of her Maori desire, our hands shot off this way and that, stroking, kneading, squeezing, penetrating, our legs rolled round each other, our thighs trapped our faces, our stomachs and biceps stiffened, the springs of the bed replied, the echoes in my bedroom too, and then, all of a sudden, Aunt Julia's superb lioness's head surged up from amid the combat zone, surrounded by its incredible mane, and her voice, now gravelly, asked me:

"What's up?"

I answered:

"Nothing."

Nothing was up. Absolutely nothing. Nothing but a pathetic little mollusc lurking inside its shell. And refusing to stick its head out. For fear of being bombed, I supposed. But I knew that I was lying to myself. In fact, my bedroom had been crowded out. Crammed full of people. All around my mattress spectators were standing to attention. And not just any sort of spectators! A whole circle of Cubans, Mois and Satares, naked or in uniform, decked with crossbows or Kalashnikovs, as bronzed as statues, covered with the dust of glory. They were all up! And, their hands on their hips, they made for a tightly packed guard of honour, hardened and curved upwards, cutting me down to size.

"Nothing," I repeated. "Nothing's up. I'm sorry."

Then, as there was nothing else I could do, I started giggling.

"And what's more, you even think it's funny, do you?"

Sometimes you laugh precisely because it isn't funny. I explained that to her. I apologized all over again. I told her that we were surrounded by a panel of Olympic judges and that I'd never been a competitive type. She said:

"I see."

Then she, too, did a bit of explaining. Our little misadventure was, in fact, to be the final stage in her investigations into primitive and revolutionary love-making which she was supposed to have ready for the next issue of *Actuel* magazine.

"Oh!" said I. "So you work for *Actuel* then, do you?"

Yes, that was indeed where she worked.

"You see what's killing love-making is the turning of love into a media product. All men would get hard-ons if they didn't know that all other men got hard-ons, too!"

I tried to caress her during her explanations, but she pushed my hand away. No second chances.

"What screws up creativity is comparison . . ."

Where was Julius? Where the hell had Julius got to? Probably in Hadouch's kitchen. Fuck life. Bombs can go off under your arse, a get-together of Indians and heroes slice your prick off right when it matters, but your favourite dog will still be calmly stuffing his face in your local eatery. Sod Julius. I knew him not. Three times over. Like Saint Peter's denial.

That was, of course, the exact moment when my bedroom door decided to fly open. Julius. Ah yes, it was Julius.

Chapter 11

But it was also Thérèse. Thérèse was standing there on the threshold, with Julius by her side. Then another head emerged: Louna. Then another: Jeremy stretched up on tip-toes. And then Clara. They didn't enter my room, but just stayed there bustling about on the threshold. Thérèse said:

"Ah! So you're alive . . ."

Perhaps, but not up and kicking.

I nodded down at my mollusc and said:

"Limping along . . ."

Thérèse grinned her chastest sardonic grin at my bedmate who, still absolutely starkers, was sitting there with her mouth agape, cut off in mid-flow.

"Aunt Julia I presume?"

There's a charming little sister for you. The little credibility I had left went straight out the window. Aunt Julia now knew that she wasn't the first Aunt Julia in my existence. If Thérèse continued in the same direction, Julia would soon know all about my scoring tactics. Ah yes! Shame on me! I used to pick up the Store's more attractive shoplifters. That was the sad truth of the matter. Men are beasts. But some men are even beastlier than me. Another man, for instance. A certain Cazeneuve. Or all other store detectives like him, who only hunted down lady shoplifters so that they could give them the choice between being fingered by the law or being fingered in the changing rooms. At least I was no rapist. I would even go so far as to say that every time I seduced an Aunt Julia, I was saving her from being violated. After which, I took whatever was on offer.

It was hard to work out whether Thérèse was pleased that I was alive or not. Her kingdom was not of this world. In a coldly clinical tone of voice she asked Aunt Julia:

"With such big bosoms, how do you manage to sleep on your stomach?"

Julia's eyes widened. It was this expression of furious amazement that was captured by the explosion of Clara's flashbulb above their heads.

Upon which, brothers, sisters and dog were pushed inside the room by a screaming horde of gatecrashers. All laughing merrily. With half-naked bodies, easily as beautiful as Julia's Satares. The whole gang leapt onto our bed and started caressing us all over. There was a series of exclamations in an unknown lingo:

"Vixi Maria, que moça linda!"

"E o rapaz também! Olha! O pelo tão branco!"

Julia made a strange face, which mingled delight and disbelief, as though the force of her frustration had just made her dreams come true.

"Parece o menino Jesus mesmo!"

This last replique was spoken with such humour that everyone laughed, even those who didn't understand. The caresses hotted up, Clara's flash sparked away, Julius tried to force his way through to his master, Jeremy's eyes were as wide as saucers, Louna was smiling like a pregnant woman, Half Pint was hopping up and down and clapping his hands, Thérèse was waiting for it all to be over, Julia was starting to return caress for caress, while I was scared shitless that a Fairy Social Worker might suddenly appear, complete with a blue-kepied Angel from the Vice Squad. But who should come in but the man behind this lovely little get-together.

"Theo!"

He was wearing a prairie-green suit. On its breast pocket there was a lettuce heart, with a rose leaf pinned in the whiteness of its centre. There was a snap of Theo in that get-up in Half Pint's album, with the following rubric: "*This is Theo going to the Teddy Bears' Picnic.*"

Giggling hysterically, he looked across at me.

"That's right! It's only me! Who does your little family turn to when they hear that their big bro's been blown to pieces? To yours truly! Unfortunately I wasn't in this evening, so they went to fetch me from the Bois de Boulogne."

"From the Bois?"

"De Boulogne. Today's the day I give my Brazilian girlfriends a picnic, to make up for the fact that they have to freeze to death there in their work clothes. When the hospital told me you were still in one piece I thought I'd bring them round for a little celebration. Affectionate, aren't they?"

(In the Bois de Boulogne . . . all my little ones . . . one day I was sure to be relieved of my big brotherly responsibilities.)

The party continued downstairs in the kids' flat with an improvized Brazilian carnival. From a neighbourhood pal, Jeremy managed to borrow a record of Ney Matogrosso, the farthest out of all of South America's multi-sexual crooners. The music blared out and Aunt Julia danced with her dreams made flesh. I drank Brazilian coffee after Brazilian coffee, under the tender stares of Theo and Clara. Jeremy followed the rhythm of the music by banging on anything noisy he could lay his hands on. Half Pint slept like all children his age sleep during a bomb blast. Louna, of course, smiled. And Thérèse, sitting on the edge of her bed, was holding the long powerful tanned palm of a huge Bahian transvestite, as dark and as gleaming as the coffee that was lining my stomach. A little bedside lamp lit up their hands and nothing else. I didn't know what our customer here was making of Thérèse's predictions, but his ecstatic eyes were glinting just as much as his lamé miniskirt. Then suddenly he leapt away from her. He pointed a trembling finger at Thérèse and started yelling:

"*Essa moça chorava na barriga da mãe.*"

Everything came to an abrupt halt, music, dancing and the coffee in my gullet.

"What did he say?"

Theo interpreted:

"He says that Thérèse cried when she was still in her mother's womb."

Flashback sixteen years and a chill gripped my soul. (I could clearly hear mum's voice saying: "The baby's crying." "The baby's crying?" "In my womb, Benjamin, I can hear it crying in my womb!")

I asked, as calmly as I could:

"So what?"

The transvestite who was dancing with Aunt Julia, the same one who had just jokingly compared me to the baby Jesus, explained in a quiet calm voice, without the slightest hint of a foreign accent:

"In our culture, Monsieur, that means she is gifted with second sight."

Then, rummaging through his strass handbag, he pulled out a statuette of bluish glass, filled with water. He knelt down in front of Thérèse and gave it to her, saying:

"Para você, mãe; um presente sagrado."

"It's a statuette of Yemanja," Theo explained. "It's their goddess of the sea. Apparently she gets them out of all sorts of problems."

The rationalist devil in me woke up and whispered in my ear:

"That's why they all end up on the game in the Bois de Boulogne."

Without a word of thanks, Thérèse accepted her statuette and went to place it on the little shelf where she kept her collection of deities.

Chapter 12

"HOW LONG WERE you in the vicinity of the pullover department?"

"For about ten minutes."

"What were you doing there?"

"I was helping a girlfriend choose a Shetland."

"Have you known her long?"

(Good old Cazeneuve, I just knew he'd survived unscathed!)

"Can I have her name and address please?"

This wasn't Inspector Caregga. It was Chief Superintendent Coudrier. At police headquarters.

Chief Superintendent Coudrier looked every inch a Chief Superintendent. He was a born, passionless looker into things. He looked into thefts, murders and now bombings, but he could easily have ended up looking into nuclear fission or a cure for cancer. It was simply the vagaries of higher education which led to him being there in front of me instead of behind a microscope. He'd been given the Légion d'Honneur, was wearing a bottle-green suit, which was not concealing a holster, and, seeing me hesitate, he explained that I was their main eye-witness and, as such, my evidence was absolutely vital.

"So, tell me about your girlfriend and the Shetland."

I replied that she was more of an acquaintance than a friend, that I called her "Aunt Julia" and that she worked for *Actuel* magazine.

Just at that moment, a door slammed, making me jump half way across the room. Damn that Brazilian coffee! It had turned me into a nervous wreck.

"Don't be so jumpy, Monsieur Malaussène. This is merely a routine questioning."

I wasn't being jumpy. I was a plucked bird on a high voltage wire, sticking its tail between its legs so that it wouldn't touch the wire opposite.

The next question sent a shock wave across the entire surface of my skin.

"And you didn't notice anything odd during those ten minutes?"

No, I didn't. I only noticed what was happening at the precise moment when *it* happened. And with a hyper-realistic accuracy. Especially the corner of that apple-green shopping bag and the two stomachs moving together. I explained all this to him. An armour-plated typewriter recorded my statement. Each burst of fire electrocuted me. Coudrier frowned and asked me:

"Could you give an accurate description of the victims?"

"Of the man I could. As for the woman, all I saw of her was her arm . . ."

I depicted the old boy as a sort of over-the-hill Roman Emperor. Claudius with one foot in the grave.

"And under his fringe of white hair, a pair of piercing blue eyes. Like Pétain."

"That's exactly it."

Then suddenly I remembered the couple kissing. The extraordinary youthfulness of their embrace.

"Are you sure?"

"Absolutely positive. Why?"

"As you will no doubt see in the newspapers, they were brother and sister."

Then he added the following point, as if it made any chance of incestuous passion impossible:

"He was a retired civil engineer for the Department of Public Works."

And then, as though talking to himself:

"Anyway, all of that is irrelevant. The victim could easily have been you."

Before adding, with a crafty stare:

"That is to say, you and your lady aunt."

Silence. The door opened. A silent secretary laid down a small tray onto the desk, just beside the green blotter. The Chief Superintendent said: "Thank you, Elisabeth," then asked:

"Coffee?"

I jumped.

"Never touch the stuff!"

While pouring himself a cup, he smiled:

"I've caught you out lying at least on that score, Monsieur Malaussène."

A master stroke. He then slowly sipped at his coffee. Its aroma went right through me. Then he put his cup back on the tray, said: "Thank you very much, Elisabeth," folded his hands in front of him, smacked his lips one more time so as to lose nothing of the aroma and stared across at me.

Elisabeth disappeared with the little tray.

"One last question, Monsieur Malaussène. What is it exactly that you do at the Store? Your statement is a little vague on that point."

It would be . . .

Oddly enough, it was just then that I took in the decor. Chief Superintendent Coudrier's office was done up in Napoleonic style. From the pseudo-Roman-looking pews our butts were perched on, to the coffee service stamped with an imperial N, including the magnificent Récamier sofa which was glimmering next to the mahogany bookcase, the whole lot being bathed in a greenish light reflected back from the spinach-coloured wall-hangings dotted with little golden bees. If I looked harder, I was sure I'd locate in that bookcase a little bust of the little Corsican, a replica of his little hat and Las Cases's memorial to him. Even though it had nothing to do with the question he'd just asked me, I wondered if this lot had been paid for out of Chief Superintendent Coudrier's own pocket, or whether he got a special police grant so that he could decorate his den to suit his whims. Either way, one thing was certain. This wasn't someone who went home every evening. It was here that he felt at home. And when you like your workplace, you like your work. This copper must have been putting in twenty-five-hour days. And you can't dally too long with a reincarnation of Fouché. All of which explains why I decided not to lie to him.

"I'm a Scapegoat, Chief Superintendent."

The Chief Superintendent's face looked completely blank.

I then explained to him that my so-called post as a Quality Controller was utter twaddle. I didn't control anything at all, for nothing could be controlled in the cornucopia of the Merchants of the Temple. Unless, that is, they employed ten times more Quality Controllers. So, whenever a customer came in belly-aching, I was summoned to the Customer Complaints Office, where I was given a complete and utter bollocking. My job consisted in swallowing this torrent of humiliating abuse while, at the same time, looking so pathetic, so witless, so absolutely desperate that the customers generally withdrew their complaints so as not to have my suicide on their consciences, allowing us then to reach an amicable agreement, with the minimum amount of hassle for the Store. There we are. That was what I was paid for. And well paid too, for that matter.

"A Scapegoat . . ."

Chief Superintendent Coudrier was still staring blankly at me. So I asked him:

"You don't have them in the force as well?"

He looked me up and down for a moment, then finally said:

"Thank you, Monsieur Malaussène. That will be all for now."

Chapter 13

WHEN I GOT outside it felt like I was walking barefoot over a bed of nails. My eyelids twitched, my hands trembled and my teeth chattered. What the bleeding hell must Yemanja put in her coffee? I just had time to drop in at home and gulp down three valiums (three valia?) before heading off for the trade union meeting which was scheduled to begin at six thirty p.m. in the staff canteen. The valium wrapped my body up in cotton wool without doing anything for the state of my nerves. Seen from the outside, I was floating, while, on the inside, I was burning up like an electric coil that was starting to frazzle.

Theo looked at me quizzically:

"Are you hurting?"

"It's more like I've O-D'd."

The meeting was in full swing. For once, the entire staff was present. Unionised or not, C.G.T. reds or in-house blacklegs, all of Sainclair's "fellow members (and memberesses) of staff" had showed up. Lecyfre, the automatic C.G.T. wisdom dispenser, was totally out of his depth. Lehmann, the apple of the bosses' eye, was hardly doing any better. Everyone was doing their pieces. There was no point in them yelling "quieten down, now, comrades!" or "order, order, my friends!" while raising their arms to try and calm the storm, they got nowhere. The panic got the better of them. Everyone was screaming out their terror, or rage, or quite simply their point of view. The clattering-cutlery pyrex-concrete acoustics of the huge canteen didn't help much either. There was such a din that you couldn't even hear the person next to you. "What if she really evicts him?" Christ knows why, but that thought suddenly gripped me. What if Louna did get an abortion? In a flash, I could see their ruined love, meaning an entire life, then, as an alternative, the same love being wrecked, gobbled up by the little competitor at Louna's breast.

"Perhaps you have your idea about all this, Malaussène?"

Lecyfre's question, coming from out of the blue, shot me down in full flight.

"Disgruntled customers, that's your line, isn't it?"

The only reason he bawled out this question was to concentrate the entire assembly on me and so make them silent. It worked. Heads were already starting to turn. So many of them, that I really did feel out on my own. Did I reckon that some customer was so disgruntled with my services that he was planting bombs under our arses? That was the question, was it?

"A quality controller must have an opinion about all this. Specially when he does such a good job as you do!"

There was, of course, no answer to that. So I didn't answer. All I did was lift a weary fist in Lecyfre's direction, from which I allowed a ready-moistened middle-finger to spring up. Lehmann had a good chuckle, and was joined by a few others. Lecyfre's smile clearly stated that he was going to get me for that. Meanwhile, he'd got the quiet he'd been looking for. Gazes started to drift away from me, with some of them dallying longer than others. Someone declared that there was no way the bombs were being planted by our normal customers. The debate moved off in a different direction. It was quite obvious that the Store was being targeted. Lecyfre and his henchmen reckoned that the problem must come from the management. Lehmann shook his head, but this didn't stop the idea from catching on. Some salesgirls demanded that there be an audit. There must have been an over-juicy fiddle going on somewhere up there which had now brought about this nemesis. Those bombs were the exploding eggs of some vengeful booby. Unless – this was Lehmann's idea – they were the beginnings of a protection racket. A racket? What racket? Had any organization claimed responsibility for the bomb (or bombs)? No, not as far as we knew. Had the management received any offers they couldn't refuse? No? So then? The racket idea was bullshit. A loner, then. Who was trying to get the Store closed down. That's what it was!

So there we were, then. That was this meeting's real agenda. What stance should the staff adopt if the management decided to shut up shop? There were loud protests left, right and centre. Unanimity. Closing was out of the question. If the Store shut, then they'd squat it. It wasn't up to the staff to pay for the management's cock-ups. OK, but what about security? Silence. Every hand dropped back down again.

"You'll see. They'll end up demanding danger money."

Theo was having a ball.

"They'll be selling knickers from behind sandbags. What a lovely war. Lehmann will be able to get back into his jungle combat uniform and we'll hand out bullet-proof vests to the customers."

Theo went on elaborating his vision, but I stopped listening to him. And started listening to something else: there, in the exact geometric centre of my brains, was a tiny ultra-sonic whistle. It was shrieking. With a noise that twisted around itself like a revolving firecracker. Then a dull ache started to spread out towards my ears. It got tenser, began to burn and I soon found myself suspended in mid-air from a white-hot steel wire which was running through my skull. The pain made me open wide my mouth, but no sound came out of it. Then it quietened down. And disappeared. Theo, who was staring at me like I was at death's door, looked relieved. He said something which I didn't hear. *I was deaf.* I answered him anyway:

"It's all right, Theo. I feel better now, thanks."

My voice came out of a microscopic deep-sea diving bell buried at the base of my heel. I gestured to Theo to pay more attention to the platform, where the debate was continuing. Mouths were opening and fingers pointing. Lecyfre and Lehmann were laying down the law. I couldn't hear a thing any more, but *I could see.* I could see all those tense backs and anxious napes. And, for the first time, I realized that I knew all those men's and women's backs and napes. I even had the strange feeling that I knew them all intimately. I could put a name to most of those fingers being raised. During the last five months that I'd spent traipsing round the Store, my eyes had taken them all in. They were now a part of me. I knew them like I knew the twenty-four thousand-odd plates in the Tintin comics, with their twenty-four thousand-odd bubbles, my homeopathic memory which brought screams of delight from Jeremy and Half Pint.

Suddenly, the four coppers scattered round the room sprang into view like lice on a shaved scalp. Nothing distinguished them from the other males there. Coppers, sales assistants and white-collar staff all had the same identity bracelets and the same creases in their kegs. What was different was their stares. The four of them were watching the others, while the others were looking forwards, pathetically, as though the promise of a new explosive-less day might suddenly dawn from the trade union table. As for the coppers, they were looking for the killer. They had a trick-cyclist's stare. You could see their ears getting bigger. They were pot-holing into the surrounding atmosphere. Who, among those there assembled, was fucked off enough to want to blow the place up? That was all they were wondering.

And they could stay wondering about it for quite some time . . .

The killer wasn't in the room! That certainty inscribed itself in letters of fire across my inter-galactic silence.

I then slid off through a side door without even attracting Theo's attention. I went down a corridor cluttered with fire extinguishers and bristling with arrows. Instead of taking the exit, I swerved left and pressed down on the bar of a door, which swung open under the pressure.

With all its lights on, the Store was slumbering in a golden glow. Even though there was total silence inside my head, I could almost hear its own majestic silence, too. Escalators that aren't escalating are more than just motionless. Counters laden down with merchandise, but with no shop assistants behind them, look more than just abandoned. Tills no longer having their bells rung are deader than the grave. All of that in a deaf man's eyes made for another world. A world in which bombs went off without leaving a trace.

"Are you looking for where to plant the next one?"

That basso-profondo voice, which I knew so well, revealed that I'd got my hearing back. Its owner leant on his elbows beside me. Instinctively, we both stared down at the Shetland sweater counter far below us. I finally answered him:

"There are so many ways to kill, Stojil, it's off-putting . . ."

Stojilkovitch was genetically Serbian, professionally a night watchman and of an age which his smile refused to make respectable. His voice was the deepest in the world. Big Ben at midnight. And it was telling me a charming little tale:

"I knew a German-killer during the war, in Zagreb. He was fifteen or sixteen, with the face of an angel, we called him Kolia and he'd found a good dozen foolproof methods. For example, he went for a stroll arm-in-arm with a pregnant accomplice who was pushing a pram. He shot an officer dead, just after mass, with a single bullet in the back of the neck then hid the still-smoking revolver next to the sleeping baby. Things like that. He gunned down eighty-three men. He never went on the run and he never got caught."

"What happened to him?"

"He went mad. To start with, he wasn't really cut out to be a killer. In the end, he couldn't stop. It was a form of psychopathic obsession that was quite common among the partisans and which greatly interested the international psychiatric community after the war."

Silence. My eyes strayed for a moment over the gilded cast-iron handrail which sealed off the new-born-baby department, just opposite me, across the void. The buggies and prams had lost their innocence.

"Fancy shoving wood around this evening?"

"Shoving wood around", in Stojil's vocabulary, meant an invitation to play a game of chess. Till midnight, every Tuesday. It was the only time that I was unfaithful to the children. Yes, shoving wood around, that evening, in the brightly lit sleep of the Store, was just the sort of chilling out I needed.

Chapter 14

THE BLOW HIT me smack in the side. I didn't even have time to get my breath back before another attack, from the front this time, floored me. The only thing I could do was curl up into as tiny a ball as possible, let the blows rain on me and wait for it to stop, even though I knew it never would. And it didn't. I was getting hit from all sides all at the same time. In my mind's eye I had a vision of a crew of American sailors whose boat had gone down somewhere in the Pacific, around the end of the war. The men in the sea had hooked their arms together to form a solid, floating mass, like a huge slick of humanity. The sharks had attacked that pancake from the edge, nibbling inwards, nibbling inwards, until they reached the centre.

That was just what Stojil was doing to me. He pushed my men back till they were around my king, then attacked from all sides at once. The way he managed to play the diagonals and perpendiculars simultaneously showed that he was in hot form. Just as well. Because when Stojil couldn't *see* his way through, then he cheated! He was the only man alive who could cheat at chess. All his pieces would leap forward two or three squares, his opponent's eyes would glaze over, the world wobble on its axis and morale drop to zero, for an out-of-focus chessboard is the real sign that moral values are dead. But that particular evening, he didn't need to cheat. He *saw it all.* He saw and I admired. All his attacks were discovered ones. A knight leapt forwards crabwise and a bishop jumped out from behind, as clean and as unexpected as a razor-blade. When the knight landed, he too stuck his fork into the cake. If I guarded my leg, my arm got gobbled up, if I stuck my head in, I smothered myself. There were no two ways about it. He was in top form. And I was the mole blinking under the owl's flashlights. In my head, the ball bearing, which had been rolling around like crazy trying to find the way out, finally went still and watched its defeat in fascination.

"There are seven of them."

He hadn't taken his eyes off the board. There was just that distant murmuring of a bass which he had instead of a voice.

Seven of them? Seven what? Or seven who?

"There are six detectives in the Store, plus our own one, so that makes seven."

Our own one, that big spotty git with salivating lips, who was nodding in admiration at each of my opponent's successful moves, stiffened noticeably.

"One in Sainclair's office going through the books, one on each floor hiding in the shadows and our one here, pretending he knows how to play chess."

Saliva Lips was too flabbergasted to get upset.

"How do you know that? You didn't even see them come in!"

Without a word of reply, Stojil switched on Miss Hamilton's microphone, the same one that summoned me ten times a day to the torture chamber, bent down over it and let his vocal chords rumble into it.

"Second floor, record department, put that cigarette out please."

I reckoned that from the tone of that celestial double bass the second floor prowler must have thought he was in direct communication with God the Father in person.

I knew my Stojil off by heart. The fact that they'd lumbered him with seven coppers hurt his pride. And then, when society starts watching its watchmen, things are turning nasty. He knew all about that already . . .

But he nevertheless went back to the game, pushed his bishop's pawn over the central line and declared:

"Mate in three."

No doubt about it. A smothered mate. Death by suffocation. Nice one, Stojil. The victor got to his feet and hauled his old bones over to the receptionist's window, from which Miss Hamilton enjoyed a panoramic view over the entire Store. Saliva Lips then went gingerly back onto the offensive. "Well then? How do you know there are seven of us?"

Stojil's lonely gaze lingered for a moment over that broad, glittering void.

"How old are you, lad?"

"I'm twenty-eight, sir."

From his quavering voice Saliva Lips sounded more like he was eighteen. But his dehydrated sparrow's bonce made him look eighty-eight.

"What did your daddy do during the war?"

Their conversation was now a parallel one, with both their gazes gliding out in formation through that vast brightly lit silence.

"He was a gendarme. In Paris."

Stojil's gaze plunged down into the guts of the Store, then suddenly swooped up again, skimming over each floor, one after the other, before turning back inside his head, as though it was making a report.

"There's a footy smell in here, don't you think so?"

The gendarme's son's ears went red. But the night watchman laid a paternal hand on his shoulder. "Don't apologize. It's me."

Then he added:

"The scent of the sentryman."

Then slowly, ponderously, Stojilkovitch started telling the little copper his life story, from his early days in a seminary when, as sentry of the soul, he'd set up a double wall of Aves and Paters around his dogmas, then his loss of faith, the defrocking, his enrolment in the Communist Party, the war, the Germans marching through the depths of the valleys, then Vlasov's armies (a million men all slaughtered with knives at the end of hostilities), parading way down there under sentryman Stojilkovitch's impassive gaze ("the guardian of the Balkan doorways into your Europe, my lad!"), soon to be followed by the liberating hordes, Tatars with their razor-sharp teeth, ear-collecting Circassian horsemen, and watch-collecting White Russians, who would dearly have liked to break through those Balkan doorways too, but that was forgetting sentryman Stojilkovitch's vigilance, steeped in the stench of his footy perspiration.

"A sentryman never looks at his feet, my lad, never!"

Lovely stuff. The Store suddenly started looking like the Grand Canyon. With Stojil watching over the world.

"I didn't let a single one in! And just as well. Because if I had let any of them in, then your tills would now be ringing up sales in rubles, and not giving back any change."

Goodness me. Seen in profile, Stojil really did look like an eagle. No spring eaglet, that was for sure, but quite something compared with that young fledgling next to him who was gobbling up his every word!

"So that is why, when I'm given a nice little place like this to guard, I can still spot eight woodlice."

"Seven," Saliva Lips said apologetically. "There are only seven of us."

"Eight. The eighth one came in five minutes ago and none of you even noticed."

"Someone came into the Store?"

"Through the fifth-floor exit which leads to the canteen. It doesn't lock. I've already reported the matter three times."

Saliva Lips didn't wait for him to finish. He leapt onto the microphone and relayed this piece of information volubly across the silence of the Grand Canyon. After which he shot off like a blue-arsed fly towards the exit in question. Springing out from behind their respective counters, the other six detectives did likewise. We enjoyed the show for a few seconds then, putting his arm around my shoulders, Stojil walked me back to the chessboard.

"You ought to get your pieces out, then support the centre, Ben. Otherwise, you'll always end up getting smothered. Look, one of your knights and one of your bishops haven't even moved."

"If I move them out too quickly, you force me into making exchanges, then do the Yugoslavian dirty on me with your pawns."

"You'll also have to learn to use them. In the end, it's the pawns that make all the difference."

That was the point we'd reached in our strategy lesson when the door of the sentry box opened and in walked Julius, tail wagging, quivering with joy at finding his master again, just like he did every Tuesday at the same time of the evening. I had never refused him that pleasure. He was still all over me when the door flew open once again:

"Hey, night watchman, you haven't got a . . ."

The copper, who broke off his question on seeing Julius, was huge, barrel-chested, with a head of black bristling hair and beetling eyebrows: like something straight out of a Mack Sennett film.

"Jesus, what the hell's that mutt doing here?"

"He's my dog," said I.

But our Law enforcer was not one for drawing out surprises. His thing was to go straight out to terrorize you, with a rolling of eyes and gnashing of teeth.

"What the hell sort of an outfit is this, with the night watchman twiddling his thumbs and people walking in and out with their dogs as they please?"

I started out to explain the wonders of chess and the importance of keeping up old habits, but he nipped me in the bud.

"And what the fuck are you doing here?"

I told him that Saliva Lips had given his permission.

"Piss off."

That was good honest authority for you. And since that was what Julius and I were about to do anyway, we pissed off on our six-footed trot back to Père-Lachaise.

"Which way are you going?"

I announced my route: the out-of-order door on the gangway.

"My arse you will! You'll go out the staff entrance like everyone else!"

We veered off. Julius and I headed down the escalator which, in five revolutions, would dump us downstairs in the toy department. Behind my back I could hear our humanist yelling:

"Pasquier, show our comedian and his toe-rag out!"

And then:

"Doesn't that mutt stink something rotten!"

Pasquier, who was already on my heels, whispered into my ear:

"Sorry, really I am . . ."

I recognised Saliva Lips' childish voice.

"That's pulling rank for you, old lad, you're quite forgiven."

In front of me, Julius cautiously negotiated the steps of the unmoving escalator. They were at an unusual height for him. His fat arse waddled between the formica sides. A sheep-shagger's delight. Delighted at finally reaching the terra firma of the ground floor, he turned round and, hopping up and down on his four legs, he gave me his celebration dance. It was true he stank something rotten. I really was going to have to give him a bath.

It happened when we got to the toy department and, for the moment, it remains my worst memory. My dog, who had got back into his elder statesman's stride, suddenly went rigid. Saliva Lips and I barged into him and almost fell flat on our faces. As we hit him, Julius wobbled and flopped onto his side, as stiff as a wooden horse. His eyes had rolled back into his head. A thick foam was pouring out from between his black chops, which were pulled up in an apocalyptic grin. His tongue was so firmly curled up in his throat that it was impossible for him to breathe. My poor Julius was puffed up fit to bust. He was like a dead horse several days after the battle. I threw myself down on him, stuck my arm into his gaping maw and pulled back his tongue like I was trying to rip it out. It finally gave way, straightened out with a crack and my dog's eyes rolled back into place. But the expression I saw in them made me spring backwards. That was when he started howling. A distant, siren-like howl which welled up and which, as it got louder, filled the whole of the Store with a terror fit to waken the dead. All the horror of the world contained in one mad dog's interminable howling.

"For Christ's sake, shut him up!"

Now it was Saliva Lips' turn to lose it. Without at first copping onto what he was doing, I watched him unbutton his jacket, snap open his holster, grab his gun then point it at my dog's head.

My foot shot out of its own accord, kicking the copper's wrist and sending the gun off to get lost somewhere in the Store. But he just stayed standing there, with his arm stuck out, like he was still carrying. Then it finally flopped down again. I seized the moment to grab hold of my dog.

He was light!

As light as if he was empty!

And he went on howling, with his mad staring eyes and grin wide enough to swallow the sky.

"And what's more, he's epileptic!"

It was DI Nasty's voice, just behind me. He'd crept down after us and was now having a good giggle.

Chapter 15

EVEN THOUGH THE coppers on duty at each entrance were doing a thorough job, the next day, the Store seemed to fill up even more quickly than ever. Every bag was searched, the depths of every pocket and every suspicious-looking bulge. A few bodies were even frisked: chest, groin, turn you round, back, rear pockets, turn you round again, then at last you'd be waved through.

The customers were obviously loving it. A little make-believe danger to whet their consuming appetites. Plus the desire to see what a store where bombs exploded looked like. The Shetland woolly counter was taken by storm. But even though their eyes swept the floor like mops, there was nothing to be seen, not a drop of blood, nor the slightest tuft of hair in the sweaters. Bugger all. Nothing had happened. Not a thing. The same old syrupy arrangement of *Singing in the Rain* was treacling over the same old counters where the same old customers were being herded together. Then four little notes – they reminded me of my boyhood and Radio Free France – and Miss Hamilton's haze:

"Monsieur Malaussène is requested at the Customer Complaints Office."

My day had begun.

I had met that girl with the placebo voice right at the beginning of my brilliant career. In the staff canteen. She was small, round and rosy. And I just knew that she had to have a real doll's arse. Specially from the way her eyelids would tilt down, closing her eyes every time she threw her pretty little head back. She was drinking some pink-coloured milk with a straw, which was presumably the secret behind her translucent petal tint. Things got off to a good start between us. They should have finished well, too. But then she asked me my name:

"Benjamin," I said.

"What a lovely name."

Strangely enough, her voice was exactly the same as her loudspeaker speak: a cloud of ether and, when you thought about it, she had the same colour as her voice. She smiled prettily at me:

"And what's your surname?"

Lecyfre, who was passing behind her, dumped my name down onto the table:

"Malaussène."

The girl's eyes widened.

"Oh, then, it's you!"

Yes, even then, it was already me.

"Sorry, but I have to get back to my microphone."

She didn't even finish her shake.

I already stank like a goat . . .

And work was just what we were to talk about in Lehmann's little turret. Sainclair was there awaiting me in person. He was sitting behind my immediate boss's desk, while Lehmann stood beside him, heels to attention, chest out, hands crossed behind his back, eyes alert. No customer. No chair for me to sit down on. Bright neon lighting. And that sweet look in Sainclair's eyes, our big boss.

"Monsieur Malaussène, quite by chance I met Chief Superintendent Coudrier at some mutual friends', and do you know what he told me?"

I noticed "chance", "mutual friends" and said to myself: you're lying, Coudrier simply phoned you up. And I answered:

"No, unfortunately I wasn't invited."

"And yet you were at the centre of our conversation, Monsieur Malaussène."

"Ah! so there is an explanation for everything," I said.

"What do you mean?"

"The dream I had last night. I was burping Moët et Chandon."

"Last night you were not dreaming, Monsieur Malaussène, you were disturbing the Store by obstructing the police and our night watchman in the execution of their duty."

(News spreads like stink.)

Lehmann frowned. Sainclair made himself look sincerely sorry.

"Things are not looking good for you, Monsieur Malaussène."

(And yet they were certainly looking brighter than they were for my dog. The night vet had snapped three needles on his reinforced concrete thigh before managing to inject him. Apparently epileptic dogs exist and he should be better by tomorrow evening. That morning he'd still been sticking his tongue out and gobbling up the world with his gaze. Still stiff. Still death-like.)

"What made you tell the police about this Scapegoat business?"

That was it. That's why Coudrier had phoned him.

"All I did was to answer his questions."

In front of Sainclair the desk was absolutely impeccable. With a turn of his little finger, he chased away an imaginary grain of dust.

"I had rather thought that we'd decided that your silence had its price, Monsieur Malaussène."

His style got my goat. I told him so. I also told him that conditions had changed quite a bit since it had started raining bombs in the Store. The police were looking for the bomber. All the staff were being combed for possible grievances. And the person getting the worst press was yours truly, because I got bollocked from dawn to dusk. So it was absolutely reasonable for me to explain the true nature of my job to our supercop, so that he wouldn't get it into his head that I spent my nights booby-trapping the Store in revenge for my "arduous daily round". (I said "arduous daily round" in true Sainclair style.)

"But that is precisely the idea you have put into his head, Monsieur Malaussène."

There was no hint of satisfaction in Sainclair's voice. He sounded sincerely sorry. He explained:

"I didn't even have to deny your story. Chief Superintendent Coudrier didn't believe a word of it. How did you expect him to? The post of 'Quality Controller' exists in all enterprises such as ours. And, given the nature of the job, it is quite natural for customers' complaints to be communicated to him . . ."

I heard him, but couldn't believe my ears. That post in this outfit was pure bullshit and he knew it. And I told him that he knew it.

"Of course it is, Monsieur Malaussène! Given the sheer quantity of articles that leave a department store each day, how can a quality controller hope to control anything? Even if one employs more of them, which is what most large sales outlets do, the percentage of complaints remains practically identical. I therefore thought it more cost effective to give the post a . . . how shall I put it? . . . 'public relations angle', an angle into which, I must say, you fit particularly well and which has the twofold advantage of reducing the number of our employees and of bringing most complaints to an amicable conclusion."

That was, indeed, his grand theory. He'd explained it to me thoroughly the day I was taken on. Why had I agreed to go along with this fiddle? For a laugh? (What a giggle . . .) Because my mother was always doing runners and being a doleboy didn't suit my role as guardian of a large family? (We were getting warm . . .) A deeply hidden part of my character? (Crap . . .) Whatever. I'd agreed to stink like a goat and it was a smell that gets up people's noses.

Sainclair must have been reading my mind, because that was where I'd got to in my stubborn silence when he set me this poser:

"Monsieur Malaussène, do you know what Clemenceau said about his principal private secretary?"

(I didn't give a toss.)

"He said: 'When I fart, he's the one that stinks.'"

Lehmann's paunch wobbled up and down convulsively. And Sainclair went on:

"Many excellent people are principal private secretaries, Monsieur Malaussène. It's a post they even struggle hard to reach!"

I just couldn't describe Sainclair. He was handsome, smooth, sweet, a success, he was like a new philosopher, a new romantic, a new after-shave, he was new, but bred up on traditional fodder. He pissed me off.

"Do not make the police think you are paranoid, Monsieur Malaussène. Imagine if they checked out your scapegoat story by questioning your colleagues? What would Chief Superintendent Coudrier find out? That the Quality Controller controls nothing. That he therefore doesn't do his job. Which explains why he is constantly being called into the Customer Complaints Office. Such are the conclusions that Chief Superintendent Coudrier will inevitably arrive at. And you must admit that that would be a pity. Because, the truth is that you do your job extremely well!"

These words (if I may coin a phrase) took mine out of my mouth. Which allowed Sainclair to press straight on:

"I had rather a hard time of it convincing Chief Superintendent Coudrier that you were joking. Take my advice, Malaussène, and don't play with fire."

I made a note of the disappearance of the "Monsieur" and then, Christ knows why, I thought of Half Pint and his Xmas Ogres, I thought of Louna's new-found loneliness, I thought of mother's endless escapades, I thought of my quick-starched dog, all of which did my head in, like a lost love, or a sudden downer, whatever, I ended up replying:

"I won't be playing with or at anything any more in your set-up, Sainclair. I'm quitting."

He sadly shook his head.

"Do you know what? The police have even thought of that possibility as well. No personnel changes are to be permitted until investigations are over. No firing and no hiring. Sorry. I would so dearly have liked to have accepted your resignation."

"You'll be even sorrier when I start wetting myself in front of the customers, when I start rolling on the ground and frothing at the mouth, or when I jump at that sack full of medals' throat and rip his tonsils out with my bare teeth."

Sainclair instinctively put a hand out to restrain Lehmann, who was no longer in a laughing mood.

"That wouldn't be a bad idea, Malaussène. The Store does rather need a guilty party right now. If you want to make yourself look like a mad bomber, then don't let me stop you."

The meeting was over. What a handsome lad was Sainclair. So youthful. So efficient. And as old as the hills. I left the room in front of him. As I put my hand onto the door handle, I turned round to set him a poser of my own:

"Tell me, Sainclair, in which Tintin story does a character leave a room and say, about another character: 'I'll get even with the old ostrich.'?"

Sainclair answered me with a beautiful childish grin:

"Doctor Müller in *Land of Black Gold.*"

That smile had to be wiped off his face.

Chapter 16

BACK HOME, I found Clara by Julius's bedside. She'd skipped school so as to watch over him all day.

"You're going to have to write me a note."

Julius was still the same as ever, laid out on his side, as stiff as a beer barrel, his legs parallel. But his heart was still beating. It was echoing away inside that empty shell. A heart transplanted by Edgar Allan Poe.

"Have you given him any water?"

"He can't keep anything down."

I stroked my dog. His fur was harsh to the touch. Like he'd been mounted by some crazed taxidermist.

"Ben?"

Clara took me by the arm, gently swivelled me around and laid her head on my chest.

"Ben, Thérèse came up to see him at lunchtime and she had a complete and utter nervous breakdown. She started rolling round the floor screaming that he could see hell. I had to get Laurent round. He gave her a jab. She's downstairs now having a rest."

Poor old Clara . . . what a lovely day spent playing hookey!

"What about the kids? Have they seen him?"

No. She'd told them to have lunch in the school canteen then stay on and do their homework. She hugged me a little closer. I gently extricated her ear, savouring the warmth of her hair against the back of my hand for a moment. I asked her:

"And how about you? Weren't you frightened?"

"Yes, to start off with I was. So I photographed him."

My ever-watchful little darling, who blanked out horror with the click of a shutter! I was now holding her at arm's length. I'd never seen such a calm expression.

"One of these days, you'll wind up selling your photos, then it'll be your turn to bring home the bacon."

It was then her turn to stare me out.

"Ben, if you're fed up with your job, don't feel that you have to keep on doing it."

(Jesus! women for you . . .)

Downstairs, Thérèse was lying flat out staring at the ceiling. I sat down by her side. I'd always found it hard giving Thérèse cuddles. It was as if the slightest touch electrocuted her. So I started off cautiously. I gave her icy forehead a peck and said, in the sweetest possible tone of voice:

"Leave it out, Thérèse. Epilepsy is an extremely common, harmless affliction which many extraordinary people suffer from. Look at Dostoevsky, for instance."

Nothing doing. I pulled free one of her hands which was clutching onto a sheet gone yellow with dried sweat. I kissed her fingers one by one and, as they relaxed, for the want of anything better to say, went on in the same vein:

"Prince Myshkin, his saintly hero, was also an epileptic! Apparently you experience an incredible feeling of well-being when the fit starts. Julius is a saintly dog, Thérèse, but he's also into physical pleasure . . ."

Talking to her about physical pleasure did seem a bit out of place, but it had the desired effect of waking her up. Her head at last flopped round towards me.

"Ben?"

"Yes, my pretty?"

"Those two dead people in the Store . . ."

(Oh, Jesus . . .)

"They were supposed to die like that."

(They were, were they?)

"They were born on April 25 1918, it said so in the newspaper. They were twins."

"Thérèse . . ."

"Listen to me, even if you don't believe me. On that day, Saturn was in conjunction with Neptune and both of them were at 90° to the sun."

"Thérèse, my angel, it isn't that I don't believe you, it's just that it's all beyond me. Please, I've had a hard day at work."

Nothing doing.

"This conjunction indicates a profoundly evil personality, inclined towards dubious or illicit practices."

("Dubious or illicit practices" wasn't a Sainclairism. It was pure Thérèse.)

"Yes, Thérèse, of course . . ."

"The 90° angle to the sun indicates the submission of the personality to the forces of evil."

Thank heavens Jeremy wasn't around!

"And the presence of the sun in the eighth house is the sign of a violent death."

She was now sitting on the edge of the bed. There was no hint of fanaticism in her voice. Just the calm erudition of a university professor.

"Thérèse, I have to go out to buy dinner."

"I'll be finished in a second. Death was to occur when Uranus the Destroyer crossed over the radical sun."

"So what?" (That just slipped out in a Jeremy tone of voice.)

"So what! So, that was what happened on February 2, the day the bomb killed them both in the Store."

QED. There we were, she was now herself again. A nervous breakdown? Never happened. She got up, tidied round our ex-shop, which hadn't been touched since that morning. Just as she was starting to make the kids' beds, an idea suddenly sprang to my mind.

"Thérèse?"

"Yes, Benjamin?"

Her hands were plumping up the pillows into that fullness which beckons sleep.

"About Julius. We'll have to keep it from the little ones. He's too much of a sight. So what happened is that he got hit by a car on his way to pick me up last night and he's been taken to a special doggy hospital. 'His condition is now satisfactory.' All right?"

"All right."

"And don't you go up and see him again either."

"Very well, Benjamin, all right."

Whenever I stroll around Belleville, no matter at what time of the day or night, I always have the feeling that I'm wandering through one of Clara's photo albums. She's photographed the entire lousy neighbourhood from every possible angle. From its old façades to its young pushers, taking in its heaps of dates and sweet peppers. She's captured the lot. It's like I was already walking down memory lane. (How many hours bunked off school did it take her to achieve all that?) She'd even recorded the voice of the muezzin opposite Amar's place. That evening, while the above-mentioned muezzin was reeling off a sura as long as the Nile, a group of Arabs and Senegalese were shooting Bellevillian crap like mad things outside the restaurant door. The dice clicked against their foreheads before springing out onto an upturned cardboard box. The atmosphere seemed a tad more charged than usual. And sure enough, no sooner had that thought occurred to me than a blade flicked out from a raised fist, while the other hand pocketed the bets. The blade wobbled against the guts of a massive Black, who was turning grey like in a comic book. But Hadouch (who was leaning against the wall of the eatery and calmly munching at a bit of liquorice) then leapt forwards. The cutting edge of his hand chopped down onto the Arab's wrist, who let go of his knife with a scream. If his wrist hadn't been fractured, then it must have been made of solid steel. Hadouch's hand dived into the Arab's pocket and re-emerged with the sum in question, a five franc coin, which he gave back to the Senegalese. Then, turning to me as I walked over towards him:

"Can you believe it, Ben? Mugging a big Black for a little piece of silver! The recession really is hitting us hard."

Then, turning back towards the lad with the knife:

"As for you, you're going back home tomorrow."

"No, Hadouch!"

It was a cry of true distress. Even more cutting than the pain in his wrist.

"Tomorrow. Go and pack your bags."

When Amar had asked me news of my family unto the seventh generation and I'd done likewise to him, I left the restaurant with my little shopping bag full of five portions of couscous and five pairs of kebabs.

"What's this hospital like?"

The kids, all done up in their spanking clean pyjamas, were out to get all the possible details. And their two big sisters, in their scented nightdresses, were listening to me as though they really wanted to believe this hospital yarn as well. "It's great. With everything that a top dog could wish for. A TV in each kennel with a specially chosen programme according to each of their personalities."

"Come off it . . ."

"Straight up."

"So what's Julius's programme, then?"

"Tex Avery."

That made Jeremy tumble out of bed.

"Can we go and see him, then? Can we go tomorrow?"

"Impossible. No kids allowed."

"Why?"

"They might infect the pooches."

And so, we managed to get through the evening. We obviously had another episode of the blood and guts soap at the Store, in which fact and fiction were copulating merrily. As for the fiction side, Sid Burns and Harry Hyena were now investigating the Paris sewers (thank you, Eugène Sue), just in case they turned out to lead straight up into the middle of the Store (thank you, Gaston Leroux). On their way, they ran into a manic depressive python which they couldn't resist adopting so as to make their homo-urbanus existences less lonesome (thank you, Ajar). That was where Jeremy thoughtfully broke in:

"Hey, Ben, your Stojil there. Is he really that hot-shit a night watchman?"

"Yup, just as hot as that."

"So that means no-one could get a bomb into the place either during the day or during the night, doesn't it?"

"That would be difficult, yes."

"Even from the sewers?"

"Even from there."

Clara got up to put Half Pint to bed, who'd already dozed off, still sitting upright on his chubby bum with his glasses perched on his nose. Thérèse was taking shorthand like she was a parliamentary reporter.

"I could do it," said Jeremy.

"How's that?"

"You'll see."

Slightly worrying, that . . .

Chapter 17

I GOT UP five or six times during the night to listen to Julius breathing. He was breathing, if you can call that breathing. It was more like lumps of air were shoving their way into his body then being expelled by a ventilator which was completely beyond his control. Breath was taking care of itself. I won't mention the smell which emerged from his gaping gargoyle on an acid trip's gob . . .

Yes, he was still very much alive!

I fought back my despair by thinking facile thoughts. For instance, I told myself that I could take advantage of the situation by giving him a good bath now that he was in no shape to leg it off and smother the entire building with lather. But I didn't find that funny. So I tried to go back to sleep. I must have succeeded because, the following morning, I woke up. Feeling like it was a dog's life, even though it was my day off.

I phoned up Louna at once.

"Is that you, Ben?"

"Yes, it's me. Can I speak to Laurent?"

Sobs on the other end. Her Laurent had slept out that night.

"Oh! He'll never come back, Ben, he never will! I can feel it!"

Panic stations. I knew fine well that if Laurent wasn't with her, then he was at the hospital. There was no cause for alarm. He'd never been able to leave her for anyone other than his patients. "Give me the number of the hospital."

"Oh, Ben, please do be nice to him. He's so miserable!"

"But I *am* nice! I've always been *nice*! Who aren't I *nice* to, for fuck's sake?"

It was the same carry-on at the hospital. No sooner had I been put through to Doctor Laurent Bourdin (my sister's only love for the past seven years) than he started reeling off a lengthy explanation of his hang-ups at becoming a daddy.

"I was expecting you to call, Ben, I knew you'd phone me and, I'm sorry, but it isn't going to make any difference, she should never have pulled that one on me, having her coil removed on the sly like that, I've never wanted a child and never will want one, she knew that, and even if I had wanted one, I still reckon that I'd have preferred just having her, all on her own, all my life, you see what I mean, and in order to have kids, you have to love yourself, and I don't love myself, not even a little bit, I've never been able to stand myself, which probably explains why I became a quack, Ben, you do understand, I don't mind her loving me, but I don't want her *reproducing* me, you can see that, can't you? Look, Ben, whatever happens, don't get it into your head that I wanted to upset the family . . ."

("Upset the family"! Jesus Christ, he was talking to me like I was the Godfather in person!)

". . . but whether she gets an abortion or not, either way, things are screwed up between us now . . ."

I waited for him to pause for breath before slipping in my question:

"Laurent, how long can an epileptic fit last?"

The pro in him switched on at once.

"You mean Julius? A few hours . . ."

"It's now been one day and two full nights."

Silence. Diagnostic cogs were beginning to spin.

"It could be tetanus. Has anyone made a loud noise near him?"

"No, apart from Thérèse having her fit, no noise at all."

"Go and slam the bedroom door. If it's tetanus, then he'll jump through the roof."

(What a delicate test.) I slammed the bedroom door. Bugger all. Julius was still a lump of marble.

"In that case, I don't know," Doctor Bourdin concluded.

("I don't know" . . . an honest quack.)

"Laurent, how long can a body stay alive without eating or drinking?"

"That depends on what's wrong. But whatever the cause, all sorts of things will become seriously damaged after a few days."

It was my turn for a think. What I came up with was as simple as despair.

"I want you to save my dog."

"I'll do everything I can, Ben."

I made myself some coffee. When I'd drunk it, I imagined the grounds oozing down the inside of my skull and tried to read Julius's future in those flowing brown pathways. I am not Thérèse, the stars aren't my bedfellows and all the grounds managed to do was serve as compost for the black geranium of my depression. And this depression brought Sainclair's beaming smile back into my thoughts and my promise to wipe it off those smug white choppers.

Yes, something was definitely going to have to be done about him. I was like Julius in that respect: I'd been shoved around all over the place but no-one had ever managed to make me stay where I didn't want to be. So Sainclair was going to have to be be dealt with. Forced into firing me from the Store! Bludgeoned into giving me the big heave-ho! (That was one person at least that I was not going to be "nice" to.) It would keep my mind off other things. The beginnings of an idea started sprouting as I slipped a leg into my trousers. It crystallized when I got to the second one. And by the time I was buttoning up my shirt, it had just about turned into the idea of the century. I was so over the moon as I laced up my shoes that they were just about fit to walk off and carry out my brilliant scheme without me. I bombed down the stairs like a typhoon, blew through the kids' room, borrowed a few of the photos Clara'd taken, then went out and dived down into the métro. It was a particularly wintry February with a particularly morose clientele. Khomenei was packing babes in arms off to the front, the Red Army was defending its Afghan brothers to the last man, Poland was changing pogroms, Pinochet was busy murdering, Reagan doing the soft soap, the Right Wing was saying it was the Left Wing's fault, the Left Wing that it was down to the recession, a piss-head had statistically proved that we were all up shit creek, Princess Caroline had refused to admit she was pregnant, the General Secretary of the Communist Party had blown into an opinion poll and ended up being breathalysed, while my good self, Père Ubu, "the living citadel", was so chuffed that I hardly noticed the stations blur past on my way to *Actuel* magazine's offices.

But my creative fervour went off the boil when I found myself in front of the office door. The snag was that I didn't know Aunt Julia's name. If I described her, I'd only end up giving the entire editorial board hard-ons. "I'm shy," I thought to myself as I took a turn round the block, looking for something next to the kerb which I was sure I'd recognise at once. And recognise it I did. Aunt Julia's lemon-yellow 4CV was parked in a delivery bay with two tickets slapped on its period windscreen. A little wog-gobbling shopkeeper was threatening to phone the cops. I suggested that he phoned the white trash in *Actuel* magazine instead and, giving him a filthy suggestive wink, I hinted that he wouldn't be disappointed if he got a good gander at the lady owner's bodywork (sic). Upon which, I opened the car door, made myself comfy and waited. Not for long. Aunt Julia was down within a minute. Even though it was cold, her body was still all there. The little shopkeeper, who had been all set to open his big gob, steadied himself on his crates, his curses frozen on his lips. Aunt Julia threw herself down behind the steering wheel and, without even looking at me, said:

"Piss off."

"I've only just got here."

As she pulled off in a storm she started explaining to me what a bastard I was, how the coppers had been to see her at the magazine, how they'd asked her endless stupid questions about the bomb blast and had then asked her if she wasn't ashamed of herself nicking pullovers in a land which already had two million unemployed, whilst she was onto a nice little earner and must be absolutely rolling in it.

At which all her workmates had started rolling round the floor and she'd blazed up and sworn to have my balls for breakfast.

She suddenly pulled straight out into the middle of the Boulevard des Eyeties and, amid a horn concerto, turned round to me:

"Really, Malaussène," (that was right, she at least knew my name) "what sort of a bloke are you? You save me from the in-house pitbull, you get me into bed but don't shag me, then you grass me up to the boys in blue! I mean, what sort of a man are you?"

(I thought of friend Cazeneuve, but kept that to myself.)

"I'm even lower than you imagine, Aunt Julia."

"Stop calling me Aunt Julia and get out of my car."

"Not before I've made you a proposition."

"Nothing doing. Just get out of my sight!"

"I've got an idea for an article for you."

"Another piece about the bombs in the Store? A good fifty of your workmates turn up in our offices every day trying to give us the inside story. Do you reckon we're *Paris Match*, or what?"

Horns were blaring left, right and centre. Julia changed into first and shot off under the nose of a wine-red copper, who noted down her number while licking his purple lips.

"It's nothing to do with the bombs. Just hear me out for five minutes and, if you're not interested, then you'll neither see hide nor hair of me again till the end of your beautiful existence."

"Two minutes!"

OK for two minutes. That was quite long enough for me to explain my job at the Store to her and get her to see just what a lovely slice of photo-journalism it would make for the distinguished rag that employed her. As I talked on, she slowed down and finally heaved to right in the middle of a pedestrian crossing, where she came to an absolutely illegal stand-still.

Then she slowly turned round towards me:

"You're a Scapegoat, then, are you?"

Her voice had got back that savannah growl which sent shivers across my skin.

"You've got it. That's my job."

"It isn't a job you've got there, Malo!" (I'd always hated people calling me "Malo".) "You're a walking piece of mythology! The foundation myth of every civilization! Do you realize that?"

(Well, well, well. What a turn up. Aunt Julia was off again.)

"Just think about Judaism, for instance, or Christianity, its squeaky-clean little brother! Malo, have you ever wondered how Yahweh, that sublime paranoid maniac, got his countless creatures on the hop? By giving them a Scapegoat on every page of his sodding testament, that's how, my little darling!"

(So I was now her little darling. How about that, Sainclair? With all that enthusiasm this was going to be one hell of an article.)

"And what about the Catholics and the Prods, how do you reckon they've been able to keep on filling up their coffers for so long? By quite simply pointing out a Goat!"

(Goodness gracious me. This bird had a cosmic theory behind every micro-event in her existence.)

"And then there are our Stalinist neighbours with their show trials. And how about us? We, who don't want to believe in anything? How do we manage not to think we're all shits? By sniffing out the goat next door, Malo." (Malo again!) "And if we didn't have any neighbours left, then we'd cut ourselves in half so as to get our own portable goats to do the stinking for us!"

I willingly overlooked her calling me Malo and admired her eagerness. It was the same Aunt Julia as on the evening we'd first met. Her eyes and mane were flashing. But, given what had already not happened, I held back. I just asked:

"So you want to do the article, then?"

"Not half! Even in my wildest moments, I've never dreamed of anything like it! Big business and its Goat, how brilliant!"

(Hear that, Sainclair?)

So, she did want to do it, then. I now had to play my cards craftily. So I craftily mumbled:

"There's just one condition."

She immediately pulled back.

"I like the idea, but I don't like conditions. If I did, I'd work for the *Figaro*."

"I provide the photographer."

"What photographer?"

"A woman. The one who took this photo."

I showed her the snap Clara had taken of the two of us after my big performance. Julia's amazed fury at Thérèse's question about the size of her breasts could clearly be read on her face. As for me, I looked every inch the quiet withdrawing type.

Chapter 18

SHE THOUGHT THE photo was pretty good. I gave it to her, with the negative as a bonus. Then I showed her the snaps of the Bois de Boulogne, Theo serving vatapa to the Brazilian transvestites, the spangled nudity of their nocturnal bodies cutting through the wispy steam rising from their plates. The joy on those faces, with their prominent cheekbones, always one notch above any heterosexual happiness.

"How did she manage to photograph all these drag queens at work?" Julia asked. "Most of them are illegal immigrants."

"She knows how to make her subjects love her, Julia. She's a real angel."

We were now purring slowly through Paris, like we were going for a spin in the country. Julia wanted me to tell her everything, about myself, about the Store, about my family and, God help me, I told her. I was still telling her over the lunch she bought me on her magazine's expense account. I told her about my mother, hooked to the wild blue yonder, about Thérèse, up in the clouds, about Half Pint and his Xmas Ogres, about Jeremy, as down-to-earth as you could get, about that little tribe I fed by bearing the original sin of our consumer society. And, when I got to Louna, and how she was wondering whether or not to hold onto the fruit of her one and only love, Aunt Julia folded her long sun-tanned hand around mine:

"Talking about to evict or not to evict, do you want to come along with me this afternoon? I've got a report to write about that very question."

The lecture hall, which we were shown into thanks to Aunt Julia's press card, was as lofty as the Elysée Palace and as glittering as the Gare de Lyon's Train Bleu restaurant. An ugliness which came down the ages and cost a fortune. The room was nearly full. It stank of big cheeses. We filtered through to the side benches, which had been set aside for the press flanking a central rostrum, which made the whole thing look like a courthouse. And there was, in fact, a sort of trial going on there. The trial of the Abortionist. At least, that was what came across from the shaved scalp which was speaking, perched up behind the huge table covered with a red velvet cloth. In front of him, the audience was listening, beside him, the other experts were listening, and Aunt Julia, who'd got her little notepad out, was listening too. As for me, I was wondering where I'd seen that large completely hairless head before, with its pointed ears, its Mussolini stare and its look of being an indestructible sixty. One thing was certain, his voice was new to me. What was more, never had my lugholes been penetrated by such cold metallic vocal chords before. But Aunt Julia was obviously familiar with both the bloke and the voice. She'd just jotted down on her notepad, in an incredibly neat hand for such an explosive personality: "Professor Leonard is still much the same." She drew a careful, schoolgirl's dash, before adding: "Still much the same wanker." Which made me listen with the rest of them.

What I seemed to understand was that this (Professor of what?) Leonard was the president of a certain *Pro-life League for the Defence of Youth*, which was sufficiently weighty in France to be able to sway the electoral balance. And that was just what was getting Leonard worked up.

"What we must be asking ourselves, while not forgetting that we are not a political party and that we are simply keeping ourselves well informed," (where had I heard that one before?) "is how pro-life Christian Frenchmen like us should vote at the next election."

(Oh, so that was all, was it . . . ?)

"Are we to back those people who, scorning our most sacred values, LEGALIZED ABORTION?"

This question was asked with such a flaming stare that a blast of hell-fire singed the audience.

"No, I do not think that we are," murmured Leonard, playing to the gallery. "I do not think that we are . . ."

(To be quite honest with you, neither did I.) I rapidly peeked over Aunt Julia's shoulder, but she hadn't jotted anything else down. When I plugged my ears back in, Bullet Head was off about immigration "which has long since gone beyond a level we can tolerate", and he reeled off all the problems caused by this menace to society "not only for our economy but also for the quality of our schools, not to mention public safety and, in particular, the safety of our daughters . . ."

Either this bloke didn't like Arabs, or he didn't trust his daughter. Whichever way, Hadouch would still smash his wrists for him. I let my attention wander so as to get a good look at the crowd. It was a real squeaky-clean set. With that resigned acceptance of wealth which centuries of sensible marriages had brought about. They were mostly women. Their hubbies were all in board meetings. Christ knows why, but it made me think about Laurent, and Louna, and how they met. She was nineteen and on her way up an escalator in the métro, he was twenty-three and on his way down. She'd just been chucked by a moron who was sold on abstractions; he was off to do his junior houseman's exam. He saw her. She saw him. And Paris came to a stand-still. He didn't go to his exam and, for an entire year, they never left their bedroom. I used to take them up little hampers full of food and books (because they did still eat. In fact, they had quite an appetite. And, between their inter-galactic voyages, they used to read to each other, sometimes even *during* them, which only goes to show that the two things aren't incompatible.) Tell me, ladies, which one of your solid-gold hubbies sacrificed an important exam for you, an entire year of his studies and a whole year's salary, just like that, for Love and for the Novel, eh? Which one?

Stop rambling, Malaussène, and take a look at the new star turn instead. Leonard the Bald had in fact just sat down to allow another professor to have his say (it was a real benchload of eggheads). When the new speaker got to his feet, he gave me quite a shock. The total opposite of the preceding one! While Leonard was compact, gleaming, perfectly turned out and deadly, this one, who said he was Professor Fraenkhel, an obstetrician (I had actually heard of his name in that field), this one, I repeat, was trembling, pained and fragile. With his knobbly bones sticking out through his lanky frame, his hair all over the place, and the look of a child who's just been caught red-handed by an adult, he looked like an over-kindly make-shift creature, produced by some Frankenstein on acid then packed off defenceless into a world which was too cruel for him.

"I'm not going to talk politics," he too declared (but, funnily enough, him I did believe), "I shall limit myself to discussing the Scriptures, and what the Church Fathers have to teach us . . ."

This sums up in a sentence what it took him a good quarter of an hour to come out with, while the audience was dozing off. It was all there: "Suffer the little children to come unto me, the camel, the rich man, and the eye of a needle, blessed are the pure in heart, let him cast the first stone who is without sin," winding up with this quote, taken from Saint Thomas or someone like that: "*It is better to be born unhealthy and deformed than never to be born at all.*"

And that's when the incident occurred.

As they say in the papers.

A tall blonde girl I hadn't noticed in the second row, wrapped up in Babylonian furs, suddenly rose to her feet like a vision of heaven, plunged her hand into her Hermès bag and pulled out something bloody and indescribable, which she then hurled at the lecturer with all the strength in her body, while squawking in a squawky accent:

"Here, cop this for something unhealthy and deformed, you fucking bastard!"

The thing flew over the first row's heads with a sponge-like squelching then hit Fraenkhel in the chest, splattering the entire distinguished rostrum with pungent-smelling blood. Fraenkhel no longer looked pained, he looked like Pain personified. But Leonard, with the hiss and the speed of a wild cat, threw his sixty years over the conference table and rushed at the girl, his eyes staring crazily and his claws out for the kill. The very second he set off, the girl leapt up onto her chair, opened wide her coat and yelled:

"Freeze, Leonard, I'm carrying!"

Leonard came to a halt in full flight. The entire rostrum screamed the same horrified scream. The girl had just unveiled the most sumptuous pregnant woman's body a pro-lifer could dream of. Naked from head to toe, blossoming and as inflated as a divine air balloon, fertility in all of its earthly exuberance.

In her schoolgirl's hand, Aunt Julia noted down that Professor Leonard had just learnt the meaning of dialectics.

Later, in the 4CV, when I pictured Fraenkhel's blooded pain once more in my mind's eye, I opined that the girl had picked the wrong target. She should have thrown her offal at Professor Leonard. He was the real big bad wolf. Julia had a quiet chuckle:

"I thought you were a masochist, Malaussène, for accepting such a warped job as a Scapegoat. But it in fact turns out that you're a bit of a saint."

Yes, that must be it.

The saint got himself dropped off at the entrance to the Store and started wandering round the ground-floor aisles. Looking for someone. Someone in particular. Who I absolutely had to find. And quickly. It was seven in the evening. (Just pray he hasn't pissed off home yet. Sweet Jesus, let him still be here. Come on, Lord, just this little favour. I've never asked for much. There's even a good chance you've never heard of me. So grant my wish, damn you! Thanks!) There he was, I could see him, just about to go round the Shetlands counter. And not a single customer in sight. What a stroke of luck. I speeded up. We bumped into each other.

"Hi there, Cazeneuve!"

I gave him a good punch in the liver, a real one, with all the weight of my body. (I'd learnt that from books.) He doubled up. I just had enough time to spring back so that he puked up only on his own shoes and not on mine as well. (The snag with saints is they can't keep it up twenty-four hours a day.)

That done, I went down to the DIY department, where I found Theo frisking his oldsters, just like every evening. They were all quietly waiting there in line. There wasn't a word of protest as Theo removed all the goods they'd pinched during the day from out of their grey smocks.

"Hi, Ben, you even working on your days off now? Sainclair'd be proud of you!"

I presented him with the photos Clara had taken in the Bois de Boulogne, and helped him put back all the shoplifted goods.

"Just imagine it! One of them even spent all day walking round with five litres of weedkiller in his pockets!"

Chapter 19

DURING THE FOLLOWING week, Aunt Julia and Clara began their piece about the Scapegoat. As for me, I went at it no holds barred. I was the most spineless, whining, suicidal creep imaginable. Not a single customer held out with a complaint. They almost wound up writing me cheques. They arrived puffed up with righteous indignation, only to leave again with the certainty that, whatever they'd been through, were going through or would, that day they'd encountered something worse: misery made man, like an updated Hoffmann tale. And at each step of their voyage of initiation into the Store, they found themselves in front of Clara's lens. She captured their fury as they stormed off towards Lehmann's office, she caught each stage of their transformation inside that office, she immortalized the expression of true humanity which lit up their faces on their way out, and she it was who snapped Lehmann and me giggling like the right couple of bastards we were after we'd pulled off our little caper. Lovely Clara, *and I never spotted her camera*!

Aunt Julia had started off by spending a few days observing me in action, but soon began to work entirely from my little sister's photos. They were a more revealing reality for her than reality itself. As the snaps piled higher, she filled up page after page of her note-pad. When she spoke to Clara, it was with an odd mixture of maternal emotion and professional amazement. She'd adopted her, as if Clara was her spiritual daughter, the fruit of her loftiest ambitions.

In the evening, there were now two note-takers while I served up the kids their slice of fiction: Thérèse on her word-plucking machine and Julia with her schoolgirl's exercise book. The photos Clara took at home weren't as good as the others.

"It's because my mind's elsewhere, Aunt Julia. I listen to Ben's stories."

Meanwhile, ever more numerous tubes were beginning to sprout over Julius's body. Some went in, while others came out: water, plasma, vitamins and ox blood in one way, urine and crap out the other way. As promised, Laurent was doing everything he could. Julius didn't give a toss. With a metaphysical stubbornness, he kept on sticking his tongue out at the world, his chops drawn up all around his murderous fangs. Sometimes, at night, it almost felt like I was sharing my room with an apocalyptic spider, particularly when the moon was full and its pallid light stretched out the shadows of his spindly legs.

"How long do you reckon he can last like that?"

"I've no idea," Laurent answered. "He's obviously out to break all the records."

Then, that motionless mass of fur started twitching from time to time, making its bottles clink, causing a wave to run through the shadows which the tubes cast on my wall. This was because we'd bought him an air-pressurized mattress, designed to prevent bed sores.

As Julius hadn't returned home, the children were getting worried about him, so I told them that he was better but the head of the clinic had asked to hold onto him for a bit so that Julius could teach his own dog all the tricks of the canine trade: how to open and close doors, snuggle up to the goodies and snub the baddies, fetch the kids from school and take them back in the métro whenever it was raining.

Louna, who'd moved back in with us after Laurent's departure, listened to my porkies with a look of amazed naivety, something I recognised from having seen it so often on our shared mother's face: she wasn't the one who was listening any more, it was the little tenant thriving away under her pullover.

* * *

As for work, Sainclair sent for me again, but this time to his own personal office ("Whisky?" "Cigar?") to congratulate me for my renewed zeal. He showed me a set of figures which revealed how much money I'd saved the Store in just the previous fortnight. A tidy sum.

"There is just one thing that bothers me, Monsieur Malaussène. How on earth do you manage to do such a thankless job so well? What's your secret? A home-grown philosophy?"

"The pay, boss. The philosophy of the big pay packet."

With an oh-so-distinguished smile, he then doubled my pay on the spot. (Just wait to see what's cooking, my dear benefactor . . .)

As for Lehmann, he just couldn't believe how close we'd just got. It was the first time that he'd actually *communicated.* I had one hell of a job ducking out of all his invitations to dinner, and others too. "I know this club and, believe you me, they give you the best blow job in town there!" Real mates, in fact. When he'd seen me chatting with Clara during an idle moment, he asked me who she was.

"She's my sister and she wants to become a shop assistant. So I'm showing her the ropes."

"I had a daughter just like her. She's dead now."

Something inside him started to tremble. He turned his face away. (Jesus Christ, not even bastards are perfect . . .)

Theo, who was neither Sainclair nor Lehmann, said nothing to start off with, then finally couldn't resist asking:

"What's all this eager-beaver bit, Ben? Are you up to something?"

"Do I ask you why you photo-booth yourself all the time?"

"No, but then I tell you!"

Cazeneuve steered clear of me and put up a straight-as-a-die front. And the sneakier I got, the more I became convinced that he was actually doing an honest job!

In Lecyfre's opinion, the rumours that had been going round for some time had now been confirmed.

"You're the management's lapdog, Malaussène. I'd always suspected you were and now you've been sniffed out."

This incredible sense of smell no doubt explained the recent success of his party during the local elections. (Sixty towns lost.) All of which didn't stop him eagerly getting his in-house Union demonstration ready for March 17 (a twice yearly ritual, organized by a party which was good at communions) in order to uphold our negotiated working conditions.

"And don't try to screw things up for us, Malaussène!"

What else? Oh yes, my bouts of deafness. That needle of fire emptied out my ears on two more occasions, like they were a lousy pair of winkles. The same phenomenon then repeated itself. I could see the Store with sub-aqua clearness: the mute smiles of the salesgirls selling themselves, their puffy legs, their tills getting jammed, their discreet nervous breakdowns; endless customers imagining new needs for themselves, their delight in front of the sheer quantity of things, sale after sale after sale; shoplifters from every walk of life, rich, poor, young, old, male, female, not to mention Theo's little old men swarming around all over the place like a load of soldierless ants. It was incredible what they managed to stuff in their pockets! And what they *constructed*, in the DIY department, softly, softly, under the shop assistants' glazed stares! A cathedral of nuts and bolts. No joke! I spotted one of them building a cathedral of nuts and bolts! Chartres, I think it was. Not a life size model, but almost. When he was missing a screw with the right thread, he'd stroll slowly over to the display case in question, pinch what he needed, then head back at the same coffin-bearer's pace. He'd set up his neo-mediaeval building site at the bottom of an escalator. When customers arrived, they were too much taken up by what they were going to buy to notice him, while those leaving were in too much of a hurry to try out their new purchases to notice him either. As for him, he noticed neither the comers nor the goers. That mild form of autism, brought on by DIY, which makes men pacific and women available.

* * *

One of my bouts of deafness hit me during an evening when I was in the middle of a game of chess with Stojil. (With Sainclair's written permission, if you don't mind!) He'd been dominating me on all fronts, but I then turned the tables on him and wiped him out in two shakes. He tried his out-of-focus chessboard bit on me in vain. Nothing doing. A massacre! With that total brutality which is typical of out-and-out victories in that subtle game.

Chapter 20

ON MARCH 17, the D-Day for our twice yearly demo to uphold our negotiated working conditions, Theo had put on a pearl-grey alpaca suit. For his buttonhole, he'd picked out a blue iris, variegated with yellow. But it wasn't for Lecyfre's parade that Theo had togged himself up . . .

While I was shedding every crocodile tear in my body in Lehmann's office (a leaking gas stove had only just stopped short of wiping out an extensive family), I spotted good old Theo hopping up and down in front of the photo booth like it was the gents.

When our couple of now thoroughly brainwashed customers left Lehmann's office, they bumped into a little old man who was tapping Theo on the shoulder. Lehmann scornfully nodded towards the scene. The oldster handed Theo a rather complex structure made of bronze. Theo curtly told him to pack his bags. The sobbing oldster then went off to hide in the nearby book department. Lehmann was about to have a good giggle, but the phone rang to inform him that our in-house demo was about to reach his floor. He swore quietly to himself.

I went out.

As soon as he saw me, Theo yelled:

"What the hell's this wanker doing? He's been in there for the last five minutes!"

Loudly enough for the "wanker" in the photo booth to hear from behind the drawn curtain.

"He's like you, Theo. He's dolling himself up."

"He should tart himself up beforehand, then. Assuming there's anything worth tarting up, that is."

It was certainly true that Theo always got himself ready beforehand. He'd turned the photo booth into a real art form. Which made it even harder for him to queue up behind customers who used the machine merely as a means of duplicating themselves.

The little oldster then had another go. He was looking absolutely forlorn. And the pleading hand he was about to lay on Theo's arm was covered with grease.

"For Christ's sake, Ben, get this oil rag out of my hair!"

I gently dragged the old boy off towards the book department, where he pointed out the object of his concern to me. Perched on a coffee-table book about ancient weaponry was an assembly of four bronze taps, linked together underneath by a particularly malignant tumour of nuts.

"It's seized up, Monsieur Malaussène."

There was a sort of poetry in that plumbing. But the old boy's hands were shaking and he must have got a couple of his screws cross-threaded. Hence the excess of oil in his attempts to unblock it. The dust jacket of the coffee-table book was blotched with brown circles. (They should clean up their weapons before photographing them . . .) That evening, Theo would discreetly dispose of the bodies of both the book and the taps. But right then, he was busy. Which is what I tried to explain as nicely as possible to our case of second childhood before heading off through the maze of shelves in search of the bookseller, Monsieur Risson. Monsieur Risson was ancient too. At least as ancient as literature itself. He was an aloof old boy who'd taken a shine to me on the basis of the fact that I could read. The granddad I'd sometimes dreamed of having when childhood started to get boring. And there Monsieur Risson was. He found what I was after with his eyes closed: the paperback reissue of good old Gadda's *That Awful Mess on Via Merulana.* As I had nothing better to look forward to, I dived into the delights of the first page. Which I knew off by heart:

"Everybody called him Don Ciccio by now. He was Officer Francesco Ingravallo, assigned to homicide; one of the youngest and, God knows why, most envied officials of the detective section: ubiquitous as the occasion required, omnipresent in all tenebrous matters."

But a din awoke me from my bliss.

Lecyfre, collecting demonstrators from the basement upwards, crossed the floor and harvested another crop of salesgirls before heading up into the heights. The organizers were trying to work the laughter and the chit-chat into the rhythm of their never-changing slogans. It was good-hearted stuff, like a scout troop, like a ritual. It didn't stretch from the Bastille to Père-Lachaise via the Place de la République, but from the toilets downstairs to the Persian rugs upstairs, straight in front of Lehmann who, safely hidden behind his plate-glass window, was fantasizing about mass extermination. What surprised me this time was that Cazeneuve had joined the ascending column. He usually steered well clear of them with a knowing sneer. But on this occasion, he was there. What was more, when passing in front of me (and as I stupidly lifted my eyes from my book – sorry, Gadda) he gave me a scornful stare full of militant conviction. It was the first time he'd looked at me for weeks. Lecyfre asked me with a guffaw why I didn't join them and most of the young women following him started splitting their sides as well. Strange laughter beneath judgmental stares. Was it because I was put out? Needed to disconnect? The sword of fire cut through my skull once more and I couldn't hear a thing. But I could still see it all, those meaningful stares and that silent laughter, Theo far away pacing up and down and adjusting the iris in his buttonhole, the little oldster fiddling around with his taps, Lecyfre who'd just picked up a check-out girl, pot-bellied from spending her life sitting down, Cazeneuve charmingly leaning over the neighbouring woman's cleavage, the disappearance of our more circumspect clientele, and the photo booth which exploded.

An explosion which unblocked both my ears. The metal casing popped apart at the joints for a split second, geysers of smoke billowed through the gaps, the curtain slapped at the air, as it did so blood and guts flew through the opening, then everything fell back into place, the booth was still there, upright, silent, still and smoking. From the fallen curtain, half a leg emerged, with a foot at the end, a foot which kicked, twitched one last time, then died. An incredibly acidic odour crept into every lung present. The demo became a real demo, utterly wild and anarchic. Theo, who'd remained standing for a moment in front of the booth, dived inside. The curtain covered half of his body, then he re-emerged, turning to face me as I rushed towards him. His alpaca suit, his face and his hands were dotted with tiny bloodstains. There were so many of them, so close together, that it looked like he was naked and covered with a monstrously freckled skin. Before I had the chance to say a word, he put his hand out to stop me:

"Don't go in there, Ben. It's not a pretty sight."

(Thanks. I had no desire whatsoever to treat myself to the sight of my third stiff.)

"But what about you, Theo? Are you all right?"

"Oh, I'm fine. Far better than him, in any case."

A drop of blood glistened on his upper lip, wobbled, then fell into the heart of his blue iris variegated with yellow.

"I always said that irises were meant to be carnivorous."

But the most surprising thing was what happened next. The demo, which had temporarily been scattered, as if it had been blown apart by the explosion, formed up again on the next floor and added Security to its agenda of Working Conditions. Was it because the fireworks hadn't been as loud as the first two times? Was it because mankind gets used to anything? The crowd of customers had stopped running after the first wave of panic. The Store didn't shut its doors. The floor we were on was closed off for the rest of the day, and that was all.

Theo was taken away by the ambulance men. I decided to go and see if he was in one piece later that evening.

People talked about the explosion.

Then talked less about it.

There was just that smell in the air, which doubled the number of customers.

* * *

That afternoon, I was called in to see Lehmann two or three times. He'd moved to Miss Hamilton's little box. If I judged right from her smiling eyes, our little Miss had finally worked out what my business really was and how heroically I carried it out. She also knew how much Sainclair appreciated me and that my bread had been multiplied by two.

Too late, my lovely. You should have fallen for me when I was still an unknown. But one day, maybe, if she asks me nicely . . .

Then I got an outside call. I shut myself up in the appropriate phone box (was shutting yourself up in phone boxes really such a good idea in the present situation?) and I said:

"Hello?"

"Ben?"

(Clara! It was Clara! My Clarinette! Why did I love that voice so much, wrap myself up in its incredible peacefulness, with never a jolt, a soft tone of snooker felt, across which her words rolled so evenly . . . Steady on now, Ben, you're verging on the incestuous! Anyway, what's all this about wrapping yourself up in the cloth off a snooker table . . . ?)

"Don't worry, darling, I'm quite all right, it was only a tiny little explosion, and this time I was wearing my suit of armour, I never go anywhere without it any more, I only take it off when I come home to give you all a hug. Honestly, it was just a teeny weeny explosion!"

"What explosion?"

Silence. (She wasn't calling me because of the explosion, then. Oh well.)

"I've got some good news for you, Ben."

"Has mum called?"

"No, mum must be getting used to the bombs."

"You've finished the article with Aunt Julia?"

"Oh no! It'll take us ages yet."

"Jeremy didn't get detention this week?"

"Oh yes he did. Four hours on Saturday. For causing havoc in Music."

"Thérèse has been converted to rationalism?"

"She's just done a tarot reading for me."

"The cards say that you'll pass your French exam?"

"The cards say that I'm in love with my older brother, but that I should watch out for a rival, a journalist who works for *Actuel*."

"Half Pint's stopped dreaming about Xmas Ogres?"

"He found a reproduction of Goya's painting 'Saturn Devouring One of his Sons' in my encyclopaedia. He thinks it's great."

"Louna's pregnancy is a phantom one?"

"She's just back from her scan."

"A boy or a girl?"

"Twins."

Silence.

"Clara, is that your good news?"

"Ben, Julius is better."

Julius was better? Julius was better! No, Julius was better? Better? Julius? Yes, Julius was better. He'd even created quite a sensation that morning by going down the five floors of our building while dragging behind him a waltzing collection of bottles, which smashed up on the stairs, one after the other, the ruptured colostomy bags spilling out what they had to spill out, with the ends of their translucent tubes making him look like a wild boar trying to beat off an attack from some jellyfish. The whole place went into panic. All the tenants locked themselves indoors, and all of Julius's stenching matter besplattered itself merrily from the top to the bottom of the stairwell.

"I would give him a bath, but it's perhaps a bit early, what do you reckon?"

"Leave the bath till later, Clara. Just tell me what happened next!"

"Nothing. He's better and that's it. He drank and ate as if he'd just come back from rather a long walk, then curled up under Half Pint's bed just like he always does at this time of the day."

"Did you ask Laurent to come by?"

"Yes."

"What did he say?"

"That Julius was better."

"No after-effects?"

"None. Oh yes! There is one little thing."

"What's that?"

"He's still sticking his tongue out."

Chapter 21

AND IT STARTED all over again. The blow hit me smack in the side. I didn't even have time to get my breath back before another attack, from the front this time, floored me. The only thing I could do was curl up into as tiny a ball as possible, let the blows rain on me and wait for it to stop, even though I knew it never would. And it didn't. And this wasn't a game of chess.

THIS ISN'T A GAME OF FUCKING CHESS!

That mute scream shot me back onto my feet. The one that was pinning me to the ground yelled out in surprise and rolled off along the pavement, then I got a clear glimpse of Cazeneuve, standing there in front of me, lifting his foot ready for another good kick in the ribs. This created a nice opening between his legs, into which my own foot ploughed, causing a dingo's screech fit to wake up the entirety of the southern hemisphere. No more Cazeneuve, but a rabbit punch knocked me forwards, my arms opened, then closed, clutching for dear life onto another body which collapsed under my weight. Back to the pavement, but this time my fall had been broken by another's form, beneath me, another person who I started hitting blindly, face, ribs, guts, and who screamed for help in a . . . sweet fucking Jesus . . . in a woman's voice! The surprise made me jerk my head up, just in time to see the arrival of a foot which sliced right into my mouth, sending me reeling away to the devil. That night, the devil was armed with rather a hefty club, which first crashed down onto my shoulder, then missed me the second time because I'd started rolling over, making violent scissor movements with my legs so as to knock over anything in range.

There was a screech of tibias, the soft thump of a heavy fall, assorted moans, then the devil's stick again, which didn't miss me this time, my poor little skull exploded, farewell life, farewell day, farewell night, even to this fucking lousy night, farewell . . .

"Ubiquitous as the occasion required, omnipresent in all tenebrous matters . . ."

If heaven, or hell, or oblivion resulted in me getting Carlo Emilio Gadda back, then long live oblivion, hell or heaven!

"A drop of coffee, please, Elisabeth."

Yes, Inspector Ingravallo (but why the hell did everybody call him Don Ciccio?) who'd taken a dive when on a special mission in Via Merulana was in dire need of a drop of coffee.

"I think he's slowly starting to come round."

Oh, slowly please, come round nice and slowly, as slowly as possible. I'd just become acquainted with grief. Carlo, don't leave me, don't let me surface, Carlo Emilio, I don't want to leave you!

"What's he saying?"

"He says that he doesn't want to leave a certain Carlo Emilio Gadda. And, to be quite frank, I understand what he means."

"An Italian?"

"The most Italian of them all, Elisabeth. Gently with the coffee, you'll choke him."

Inspector Ingravallo dipped his quill into his cappuccino, hence the calm excitability of his language . . .

"It's a polydialectical language. Yes, it's rather a pity that we have no equivalent in our own literature."

I was going to have to read it to the kids, even if they didn't understand a word of it, I was going to have to get Clara ready for her exam – not for her life, she was taking care of that herself – just for her exam.

"I think he's definitely breaking surface. Help me to sit him up, will you?"

How can you sit up an accordion of aches? Julius in one piece and me in eighty thousand! How can you sit up eighty thousand pieces?

"Gently, Elisabeth, hand me another cushion . . ."

But Julius was better.

JULIUS IS BETTER!

"Who is this Julius, Monsieur Malaussène? Gadda I know, but Julius . . ."

Chief Superintendent Coudrier's question, although asked with a smile, called for an answer which would go down in his casebook.

"He's my dog. He's better."

Récamier First Empire divans don't make for the most comfortable of stretchers.

"Here, have another drop of coffee. I am no doctor, but I have unshakeable faith in Elisabeth's coffee. Help him, Elisabeth, will you?"

Yes, help me, Elisabeth. I'm sitting on my bones.

"There."

(There there, there there . . .)

"Why are Récamier divans so hard?"

"Because victors lose their empires when they fall asleep on sofas, Monsieur Malaussène."

"They lose them anyway, on the sofa of time . . ."

"It sounds as if you're feeling better."

I turned round towards Chief Superintendent Coudrier, who was sitting by my side. I lifted my head towards Elisabeth, who was leaning over me, a coffee cup in her hand (a small cup, ringed with gold and stamped with an imperial N). I lowered my head towards my feet way down there. My head went up and down. I was feeling better.

"We can now have a little chat."

Let's.

"Do you have any idea what happened to you?"

"The Store fell on my head."

"And why do you think it did that?"

Why? Cazeneuve's unjustifiable hatred? But he wasn't alone. There was at least one woman in the gang. (A woman who I punched, sweet Jesus!) So why? Because I hadn't joined the demo? No, we weren't among the Yanks, nor indeed among the Soviets. Which was one of the reasons why I didn't feel the need to demonstrate. So why had they beaten me up?

"I don't know."

"I do."

Chief Superintendent Coudrier stood up in the green light of his office.

"That will be all, Elisabeth."

Elisabeth got the message. The door closed behind her. No more coffee. Standing in front of his bookcase, Chief Superintendent Coudrier recited:

"Ubiquitous as the occasion required, omnipresent in all tenebrous matters . . ."

"Gadda."

"Gadda and *you*, Monsieur Malaussène. You were present on the scene of the first, second and third explosions. That's quite enough for some people to get ideas into their heads."

True enough. But if I remembered rightly, Cazeneuve had been there each of the three times as well. Should I say so or not? Too bad for Cazeneuve. I said so.

"That's correct," the Chief Superintendent replied. "But he did not attend Professor Leonard's lecture."

Bullet Head? What had old Bullet Head got to do with it all?

"He was today's victim."

Oh! Right.

"What were you doing at that lecture?"

It was OK to grass up Cazeneuve, but not Aunt Julia (hang on though, if they saw me, they obviously saw me with her).

"I have a pregnant sister, who's been wondering whether or not to . . ."

"I see."

Which didn't mean that he approved. Nor that he was satisfied with my answer. Just to see how I was doing, I decided to try the sitting position. Ouch! I was as stiff as Julius had been in his stiffness. (Julius was better!)

"You have two fractured ribs. You've been strapped up."

"And my head?"

"A few bumps, that's all."

(That was all.)

He walked to the other side of his desk, he sat down, he switched his lamp on. As I blinked with pain, he turned it down. So far as I could see, that rheostat was, along with the telephone, the only concession to modernity in his office. He scratched behind his ear, then his nostril, before finally clasping his hands in front of him and saying:

"You have a strange job, Monsieur Malaussène, one that must lead, sooner or later, to blows."

(Well, well, well. Contrary to what Sainclair told me, he really had believed my Scapegoat story!)

There then followed the most astonishing question that any suspect, if suspect I was, had ever heard a copper pronounce:

"Have you been setting off those bombs, Monsieur Malaussène?"

"No."

"Do you know who has been?"

"No."

Another scratching of his nose, another clasping of his hands, and yet another surprise:

"Even though I am not obliged to inform you of my personal conclusions, I should like to tell you that I believe you."

(Just as well for yours truly.)

"But in your place of work, many of your colleagues think it was you."

"Including those who jumped me this evening?"

"Among others."

The twitching of his eyebrows suggested that he was about to try and express himself clearly.

"You see, the Scapegoat is not merely the person who, whenever necessary, pays for the others. He is also, and above all, *a basic explanation*, Monsieur Malaussène."

(So, I was a "basic explanation", then, was I?)

"He is the mysterious, but also *patent* cause of any unexplained occurrence."

(And to top off everything, I was also a "patent cause"!)

"Which goes to explain the massacre of the Jews during the great plagues of the Middle Ages."

(But we were no longer in the Middle Ages, were we?)

"In some of your colleagues' opinion, you, as the Scapegoat, are also the bomber, for the single and unique reason that they *need* a cause. It reassures them."

(Well it certainly didn't me.)

"They have no need of proof. Their certainty is quite sufficient. And they will attack you again, if I don't sort the matter out."

(Sort it out, then!)

"Very good. Now, let us change the subject."

So we changed the subject to my good self. From every possible angle. Why hadn't I made full use of my law degree? (He was one of the few people in the world who knew I was the proud owner of that particular scrap of paper.) Why? Well, I didn't really know why. An adolescent fear of settling down, perhaps, of being "part of the system", as they used to say – even though I'd never gone in too much for that line of bullshit. Nothing of any interest, in fact.

"Have you ever been an active member of any organization?"

Neither active nor inactive. In the days when I used to have friends, they took care of that for me, exchanging friendship for solidarity, pinball for the roneo, evenings out for sit-ins, moonlight walks for throwing paving stones, Gadda for Gramsci. Whether they were right, or whether I was, is a question that can't be answered by any of those people who suppose that they can. And then, what was more, my mother was already doing runners, the kids left at home, Louna with her adolescent love affairs, Thérèse who was waking up the entirety of Belleville with her nightmares, and Clara who took two hours to get home from the nursery school which was three hundred yards down the road. ("I keep looking at things, Ben. I like that." Already.)

"And your father?"

One of mother's boyfriends. The first one. She was fourteen. Never met him: weep, Chief Superintendent. He didn't weep, he recorded it all, filed it away, wouldn't forget a thing.

Then came the thorny question of Aunt Julia and what she "meant" to me. What did she "mean" to me in fact? Apart from that terrible moment of acknowledged sexual failure. And the article she was writing. But that was none of his business.

"It's a little too early to answer that."

"Or a little too late."

At that, he turned up his rheostat a notch so that I could get a good look at just how serious the expression was that he'd put on his face.

"Beware of that lady, Monsieur Malaussène, do not allow yourself to be talked into taking part in . . ." (A moment's reflection.) ". . . something you might well regret."

(Hear no evil, speak no evil.)

"Journalists are terrible ones for the spontaneous act, without thinking out the consequences. While people like us realize that spontaneity is a question of education."

"Us? What do you mean 'people like us'?"

(That one just slipped out.)

"You are the head of a family, aren't you? And, in that case, you are an educator. So am I, in my own way."

Upon which, he gave me his conclusions all over again. No, he didn't think I was the bomber. But it did have to be admitted that bombs went off wherever I happened to be. Therefore, someone was trying to frame me. Who? A mystery. This was merely a hypothesis. A hypothesis which would eventually turn out either to be right, or wrong.

"Eventually?"

"When the next bomb explodes, Monsieur Malaussène!"

Brilliant. So what if the next one blew us all away? A sly question. Which I asked him.

"Our laboratories do not think it will. And neither do I."

* * *

The session ended with a few suggestions from Chief Superintendent Coudrier. Which were, in fact, orders: I was to take a couple of days off to mend, then go back to the Store. I was to change nothing about my usual to-ings and fro-ings. Two specialists would be keeping their eyes on me from dawn to dusk. Anyone who came near me would immediately be mentally photographed by those walking cameras. His two coppers would be a sort of telescopic sight and me the target. So did I agree to that? Christ knows why, but I did.

"Good, then I'll have someone take you home."

He pressed a small button (yet another concession to modernity) and asked Elisabeth if she would be so good as to send in Inspector Caregga. (Oh yes, old Turkish coffee!)

"One last thing, Monsieur Malaussène. The question of who assaulted you. They would have killed you if one of my men hadn't been there. Do you want to press charges? I have a list of their names here."

He took a piece of paper out from under his blotter and handed it over to me. I felt incredibly tempted to read it. And having that gang of silly buggers sent down was extraordinarily tempting, too. But *vade retro Satanas*. The white-draped angel in me answered "no", while saying to himself that angels were jerks.

"As you see fit. In any case, they will be charged with causing an affray and will have to answer to the Store's management, who have been informed."

None of which was going to reinforce my ribs.

Chapter 22

PARIS WAS DOZING and Inspector Caregga was driving just the way all the coppers in the world type: with two fingers. And still hibernating in his fur-collared pilot's jacket. I asked him if he could make a detour via Theo's place. So he detoured.

I set off to leap up the stairs in my mate's building three at a time, but it turned out to be a third at a time, with a stay in intensive care on each landing. When I finally got to his door it was to find a little photograph which Theo'd stuck up on it, depicting him wearing a housewife's pinny decorated with a sprig of four daisies. Apparently he wasn't in. He was round at my place. The kids must have got worried and phoned him and he must have gone round to play nanny. When I got back down to Inspector Caregga in his car, he'd almost reached retirement age. To make up for this slight delay, I had him drop me off at the corner of Rue de la Roquette and Rue de la Folie-Régnault, about fifty yards from home. This saved him from having to go all the way round via the boulevard. He thanked me, as he was on duty that evening and in a hurry. I extracted myself from the car and dragged my bones off towards the kids. The kids . . . my kids. A warm moment which, oddly enough, made me think of Professor Leonard. Well then, it had so fallen out that Pro-life Leo had managed to get himself blown away in my place of work! Funny that, because he certainly hadn't looked like someone who shops in department stores. And even less like someone who messes around in photo booths. Professor Leonard had been an out-and-out bespoke man. When I saw him at that lecture, there was a good two or three grands' worth of threads on his back, at the very least. His right shoe had obviously not been made by the same craftsman as the left one; each of them being the work of a lifetime. No, someone like that definitely didn't hang around department stores. If ever he went down into the underground, then it was because he was wandering around witless. Or else to carry out some forfeit he'd been given at his daughter's last charades party.

(Jesus Christ, was fifty yards really that far?)

Leonard . . . Professor Leonard . . . He wasn't exactly out of the same mould as Sainclair. It hadn't been necessary to teach him about tradition. No, he'd been born to it. He'd sucked in his eternal values at the breast of a pure country-bred wet-nurse. There were probably a dozen generations of qualified doctors behind him. Once upon a time they'd have been royal physicians, now they were Presidents of the State Commission, or something like that. The cream of the medical cream since Hippocrates. A man like that, a victim of fate like that, in such a public place, along with a garage mechanic from Courbevoie and an engineer for the Department of Public Works, who was in love with his twin sister! What a let-down! . . . he must be the black sheep of the family! They'd bury him on the quiet one moonless night.

(Was that really only fifty yards?)

Stop talking crap, Malaussène. You're just a little shit who knows nothing about the Top Drawer. You're judgmental and talking like a lefty. Adaptability is their real secret. Adaptability is what lies behind their power. They adapt. They become presidents by playing the accordion. If they don't take the métro, then it's because they just stroll down the Champs Elysées like kings.

Savile Row above, reach-me-downs below . . . Adaptability . . .

Theo was indeed at my place. So was Clara. And Thérèse. And Jeremy. And Half Pint. And Louna. And her belly. And Julius. Who stuck his tongue out at me. My very own loved ones.

"Ben!"

Someone shouted that. Then there was silence. A cry of pain from one of my sisters when she'd seen me. Which one? Louna had covered her mouth with both hands. Thérèse, sitting behind her desk, was looking at me like I was one of the living dead. (Which I was.) And Clara, standing up, had her eyes brimming with tears. Then her hand fumbled behind her back, located the Leica and lifted it up to her right eye. FLASH! Which dammed up the flow of horror and stopped my gob from reaching Elephant Man proportions.

Jeremy was the one who finally made everything go back to normal by asking:

"Hey, Ben? Can you tell me why we have to agree our fucking past participles with direct bleeding objects when they come before the sodding auxiliary *être*?"

"*Avoir*, Jeremy, before the auxiliary *avoir*."

"Whatever. Either way, Theo can't bleeding well explain why."

"I stick to mechanics . . ." said Theo, gesturing evasively.

So I explained. I explained that venerable old grammar rule while placing a paternal kiss on each forehead. You see, what happened was that direct objects used to agree with past participles no matter whether they came before or after the auxiliary *avoir*. But people failed to make the agreement so often when it came after that our grammatical law-makers turned the mistake into a rule. That's why. That's how it is. Languages evolve with our laziness. How "appalling". Oh yes.

"It happened downstairs from my place, Ben. They must have guessed you'd come round to see how I was doing. They jumped you just outside the door to my building."

I was lying on my bed. Julius, who was sitting on the floor, had laid his head on my stomach. A good inch and a half of floppy, warm, (living!) tongue were resting on my pyjamas. Theo was pacing up and down. "When I got back from the hospital, it was all over. A big muscly copper, done up like a Second-World-War fighter pilot, was putting you into his motor."

(Thank you, Inspector Caregga.)

"If you ask me, he was tailing you. When he saw you go into my block, he probably took the chance to go off and buy a packet of fags.

And when he came back, our friends had already been in business for quite some time."

"Did you see who it was?"

"Not a thing. An ambulance was taking away the ones in the gang who'd been nobbled by our fighter pilot. And, if you ask me, he didn't pull his punches."

(Thanks again, Caregga.)

"What about you, Theo? Nothing broken?"

"My suit's fucked."

He stopped dead in his tracks then turned towards me.

"Can I ask you a question, Ben?"

"Fire away."

"Are you involved in this bombing business?"

Now, that did put me a teensy bit out.

"No."

"Shame."

My evening's conversations were decidedly getting more and more weird.

"Because if you were, I'd not be far from reckoning you were a national hero!"

What the hell was up with him? He surely wasn't going to lay the filthy consumer society bullshit on me, was he? Not him, not with me, not at our ages, not with our jobs!

"Out with it, Theo. What's up your sleeve?"

He came over to me, sat down next to Julius's head, whose eye swivelled round (alive, Julius!) and adopted the air of a Shakespearean stage whisperer.

"The bloke who got blown away in the photo booth . . ."

Rhubarb, rhubarb . . .

"What about him, Theo?"

"He was an absolute fucking bastard!"

Be serious. That didn't exactly make him a member of an endangered species. And this bastard did have an excuse. It was his duty to be one.

"Did you know him?"

"No, but I know what he did as a hobby."

"Wanking in photo booths?"

His eyes suddenly lit up.

"Spot on, Ben."

I couldn't see anything particularly monstrous about that (or anything particularly exciting, either).

"While looking at his little souvenirs."

His voice had suddenly started to wobble. Wobbling with a fury I'd never seen in him before.

"Come on, Theo, spill the beans!"

He stood up, took off his daisy pinny, took a wallet out from his jacket pocket, removed what looked like an old photograph from it and handed it to me.

"Take a look at that."

Sure enough, it was an ancient black-and-white photo with crinkle-cut edges. Very black. Extremely black. You could make out Professor Leonard's athletic frame of about twenty or thirty years before, naked from his toes to the tip of his pointed skull, standing upright, his eyes on fire, his face twisted into a devilish grin, his arms stretched out, pinning another body down onto a table . . .

"Oh no! . . ."

I lifted my eyes up. Theo's face was running with tears.

"He's dead, Ben."

I looked at the photo again. What makes us instinctively know that a watch has stopped, even if it's telling the right time? The child being held down onto the table by Professor Leonard was dead, there could be no doubt about that.

"Where did you find it?"

"In the booth. He was still holding it in his hand."

A long silence, during which I took another good look at the photo. There was the naked man, his muscles tensed, gleaming like bolts of lightning (reflections from the flashbulb off his sweat, presumably). On what was probably a table, there was the white figure of the child, his legs dangling in mid-air. And, by the table leg . . .

"What's that there, by the table leg?"

Theo put the photo under my bedside lamp and wiped his cheeks with the back of his hand.

"I don't know, clothes maybe, a pile of clothes . . ."

Yes, a pile of something that faded away into the deepening monochrome shadows until, from that vibrant blackness, the white form of the slaughtered child sprang out.

"Why didn't you give this to the police?"

"And let them catch the bloke who killed this shit-head. No way!"

"But it was a coincidence, Theo. It could easily have been you or me."

No sooner had I said that, than I no longer quite believed it.

"Let's just say that I don't want them to imprison coincidences like that, Ben."

"Leave the photo here, don't go walking around with it on you."

After Theo'd gone and the photo had been stashed away in the drawer of my bedside table, I went to sleep. Like a falling stone. When I hit the bottom, a gorilla with a gob like an incinerator was making a fricassee of little children, who were sizzling away in his pan. That was when the Xmas Ogres made their entrance. The Xmas Ogres . . .

Chapter 23

"FACE TO FACE WITH HIS OWN DEATH!" the next day's headlines screamed, followed by four blow-ups of photo booth snaps which took up the entirety of the page (Christ, that's right, the machine had still been working!). The last four close-ups of Professor Leonard.

With his shaved head and plucked eyebrows, he was more than just bald. His forehead was high and smooth over the pronounced arch of his orbits, his ears pointed, his jaws powerful below his chubby cheeks, his complexion pale, but that might have been because of the lighting. (Another feeling that I'd seen that face somewhere before.) In the first photo, his head was slightly thrown back, his straight lipless mouth looking like a scar at the bottom of his face. Beneath his heavy eyelids, his stare was dark, cold, utterly expressionless and disquietingly deep. The overall impression was of rigidity, not because he had nothing to express, but because he'd decided to express nothing. In the second photo, the whole of that powerful edifice of fat and muscle looked like it was in the grip of an earthquake, his eyelids were raised, revealing his irises in their entirety, pierced with pupils whose absolute darkness irresistibly drew your eyes. There was a sketch of a grin on his lips, a grin which dug out two dimples that swallowed up the fleshiness of his cheeks. In the third photo, his face was breaking up. The pointed arches of his eyebrows were subsiding, his forehead and skull had shock waves running over them, his pupils had gobbled up his irises, his mouth was a diagonal crevice cutting his face in half, his cheeks had apparently been sucked away, what looked like a set of false teeth had been blown forwards, the whole thing was out of focus. The last photo was of a dead man. At least, from what could be seen of him. After the explosion, he must have slumped down on the swivelling stool. All that was visible was his left eye socket, empty and bloody. Part of his scalp had been torn away.

The head that was then being tended by Clara hardly looked any better.

"Easy does it with the lint. I feel like asparagus being parboiled."

"They're barely lukewarm, Benjamin."

My heart always misses a beat when my little sister calls me Benjamin. It was as if she was stretching out my first name so as to dam up an overflow of tenderness.

"They really did give you one hell of a facelift."

"That's nothing. You haven't seen what the inside looks like . . . What's your opinion of these photos?"

Clara leant over the newspaper and gave me her answer. It was precise. It was technical. It was her eyes talking:

"I think these journalists have written a load of old rubbish. He wasn't face to face with his own death (anyway, bombs don't kill you in four phases). He was looking at something else, something he was holding at arm's length, just below the lens."

(How right you are, my Clarinette, how right you are . . .)

"The shudders on his face happened *before* the explosion, Ben."

(That's right! That's right!)

"As for his expression, it isn't a look of pain, but of pleasure."

At that moment I gave my little sister a long hard look. I had a tiny sip of coffee, waited for it to radiate through me, then asked her:

"Tell me something. If you saw a photo that was really horrible, something you couldn't look at for very long, what would you do?"

She got up, put her big fat French literature anthology in her bag, picked up her moped helmet, gave me a cautious kiss, then, on the threshold of the door, just before going out, she answered me:

"I don't know. I suppose I'd probably photograph it."

* * *

It was at five o'clock that afternoon, when Thérèse came home, that I finally worked out who Professor Leonard's lovely gruesome gob reminded me of, why I had that feeling of *déjà vu* . . . "It's him, Ben, it's him, it's him!"

Thérèse stood there in front of Julius and me, holding the newspaper and trembling all over. Her voice was shaking with that terrible fervour which meant a major crisis was on its way. So I asked her, as nicely as I could:

"Who, him?"

"*Him!*" she yelled, handing me a book she'd just pulled out of her bookcase.

"Aleister Crowley!"

(Ah yes! Aleister Crowley, the famous English magician and bosom pal of Beelzebub, Leamington 1875–Hastings 1947. I'd heard of him . . .)

The book was open showing a photograph which was extremely similar to the first of the four photos of Leonard. A very close likeness. Beneath the photo was the following caption:

Aleister Crowley, 666, The Beast.

And on the facing page, this text which stank of brimstone:

> *The only law is: Do what thou wilt. For each man is a star. But the majority do not know this. Even the most hardened atheists are merely Christianity's bastards. The only man who dared to say: "I am God" died mad, rocked by his dear mother who was armed with a crucifix. His name was Friedrich Nietzsche. Those others, our Twentieth Century's humanoids, have replaced Jesus Christ by Mammon and celebrations by world wars. How proud they are to have fallen even lower than their predecessors. After those sublime abortions, come sordid abortions. After the kingdom of the too human human, the dictatorship of the infra-human . . .*

"He isn't dead, Ben, he isn't dead, he's been reincarnated!"

There we were. She was off.

"Calm down, sweetheart. He's as dead as a doornail. Blown to smithereens in that photo booth."

"No, he's vanished once more behind a *seeming* death so he can re-emerge all the more easily and continue his works."

(In my mind's eye, I could see that photograph of dead flesh. "His works"! I was starting to get cross.)

"Look, Ben! He went by the name of 'Leonard'!"

Her blood and her voice had both vanished behind a pallid terror. Like in a movie, the newspaper dropped from her hands and she repeated:

"Leonard . . ."

Julius's tongue was sticking out.

"Yes, his name was Leonard. So what?"

I knew it. I was starting to get worked up.

"So what? That's the name they give to the Devil on Sabbath nights, that's what. The Devil, Ben! Mammon! Lucifer!"

I knew it. I was now steaming.

I calmly got to my feet, with the Crowley book in my hand. It was a green leather-bound thing, stamped with a golden sign, a sort of Library of Other World Classics (I'd let Thérèse pile up tons of this stuff on her bookshelves, some "educator" I turned out to be!), I ripped it in two without saying a word and flung both halves away across the flat. Having done that, I grabbed my poor sister Thérèse by the shoulders, shook her gently, to start off with, then more and more violently, explaining to her calmly, to start off with, then more and more hysterically, that I'd had it up to here with her astro-forecasting bullshit and her two-bit Satan bollocks, that I didn't want to hear another word about it, that it was an appalling example to Half Pint ("appalling", oh yes, I said "appalling"), that if she came out with any more of it, even once, *even once*, then I'd beat the silly bitch to within an inch of eternity.

And, as though that wasn't enough, I laid into her bookcase, sweeping the lot away with both hands: books, lucky charms and statuettes of all persuasions went shooting over Julius's head and exploded into lumps of polychrome plaster against the walls of the flat, until even the Brazilian drag-queens' Yemanja had given up her Bahian ghost at the feet of terrified Thérèse.

I then found myself outside, with my dog. Outside, in the street. I walked like a zombie towards Half Pint's school, with an overwhelming desire to give him a hug, him and his rose-tinted glasses, to tell him the loveliest story imaginable (no unhappiness anywhere, neither at the beginning, nor at the end) and, as I walked, I tried to think of one (sweetness and light, all well with the world), and I couldn't find one, not in the whole of our fucking realism-riddled literature with its deaths, nights, ogres and foul goblins! The passers-by turned round to stare at the loony with the dented skull and the dog who was sticking out its tongue. But our passers-by didn't know any more perfect fairy stories than I did! What's more, they didn't give a toss! They were laughing with the carnivorous laughter of ignorance, the ferocious laughter of the thousand-toothed sheep!

Then suddenly my anger subsided. A tiny little round thing, squinting behind its rose-tinted glasses, had just leapt into my arms.

"Ben! Ben! The teacher taught us a lovely poem today!"

(At last! A breath of fresh air! Good old teacher!)

"Can you recite it to me?"

Half Pint folded his arms around my neck and recited his lovely poem to me, just as all the world's Half Pints recite, like pearl-fishermen, without once pausing for breath:

Tom he was a piper's son,
He learnt to play when he was young,
So his father put him on the street
To earn enough for them to eat.

But the only tune that Tom could play
Was "Over the Hills and Far Away".
The people thought his song was tripe,
So beat up Tom and broke his pipe.

So Tom, Tom the piper's son
Stole a pig and away did run.
But a copper caught him as he fled
And whipped him till he was almost dead.

His father said "There's still a way
That you can feed your dad today."
So he chopped poor Tom straight into two
And made him into a piping stew.

All right. All right. I got the message. I reckoned I'd had about enough for one day. Beddy-byes time.

And little Half Pint smiling delightedly at me from behind his rose-tinted glasses.

Smiling.

From behind his rose-tinted glasses.

Delightedly.

Children are cretins. Like the angels.

I got into bed running one hell of a temperature. All lights out. No-one permitted to come and see me. Not even Julius. When Clara started to insist, I told her to go off and comfort Thérèse instead.

"Thérèse? Why, whatever's wrong with her? She's absolutely fine!"

(Which only goes to show you should never exaggerate the ill you do to others. Leave them the pleasure of doing that themselves.)

"Clara? Tell your sister that I don't want to hear another word about her magic. Unless, that is, she gives me the first three horses at Longchamps. In the right order!"

Then the hour for feverish self-criticism arrived. What the hell did you think you were playing at? You were letting your littlest brother amass a detailed iconography of the gay underworld, the next one in line was screwing up at school, spoke like a fishwife and you didn't give a damn; you were talking your angel of a sister into photographing the worst things imaginable instead of revising for her exam; the other one's star-bothering had had your blessing for years, you hadn't even been capable of advising Louna, and here you were, suddenly wallowing in the moral crisis of the century, doing the Spanish Inquisition bit, right down to the destruction of idols and excommunication of the whole of the human race! What was up with you? What the hell was going on?

I knew what it was. I knew what was going on. A photo had come into my life. The cautionary tale had become a living reality.

Xmas Ogres . . .

It was at the precise moment when I was making that earth-shattering discovery that my bedroom door opened.

"Eh?"

Aunt Julia was standing on the threshold. A smile fluttering on her lips. I was never going to tire of describing her clothes. On that occasion, she was wearing a dress of undyed wool which crossed over the fullness of her breasts. Weight on weight. Warmth on warmth. Such a supple heaviness . . .

"May I?"

Before I'd had time to answer, she was already sitting beside me.

"Congratulations. Your little workmates really did a good job on you!"

Behind Julia's presence, I could sense Clara ("why don't you go upstairs and make sure Benjamin isn't dying?").

"Nothing broken?"

The hand that Julia laid on my forehead was cool. She burnt herself, but didn't take it away again.

I asked her:

"Julia, what do you think about ogres?"

"From what viewpoint? Mythological? Anthropological? Psychoanalytical? Folklorical? Or how about a cocktail with a dash of each?"

I was in no laughing mood.

"Cut the crap, Julia. Forget all the theories and tell me what *you* think about ogres."

Her sparkling eyes became thoughtful for a moment, then a broad grin gave me a panoramic view of her teeth. She suddenly bent down and whispered right into my ear:

"In Spanish *comer* means 'to love'."

In the rapidity of her gesture, a breast had escaped from her dress. And, since in Spanish, "to eat" was the same as "to love" . . .

Chapter 24

"MONSIEUR MALAUSSÈNE, I thought it appropriate to address you in the presence of your colleagues."

Sainclair indicated Lecyfre and Lehmann, who were standing at either side of his desk.

"So that everyone's positions may be made perfectly clear."

Silence. (Aunt Julia and I had just spent three days in bed. To my mind, every position was glorious.)

"We may not be all in the same camp, but this was definitely not a democratic way of sorting things out." Lecyfre stated his position with all the sympathy his antipathy was capable of. (Julia's hands and her hair were still running over my skin.)

"All the same, if I lay my hands on one of those bastards . . ."

That was Lehmann's vengeance speech. (Whenever I solidified again, she would deliciously melt.)

"It was a totally unjustifiable assault, Monsieur Malaussène. Fortunately, you are not pressing charges, otherwise . . ." ("God, you're beautiful! God you're beautiful! Oh my ecstatic love . . . my desire leaping forth like Haminabab's chariot!")

"And even more fortunately, I see that you have almost recovered. Your face does, of course, still bear the marks . . ."

(Three days. Let's see. Three days multiplied by twelve makes thirty-six. At least thirty-six times, Jesus!)

"But now you will really look the part in the eyes of our customers!"

This last observation from Sainclair raised a laugh from the other two. I woke up and joined in. Just in case.

* * *

So, it was back to work after four days' sick leave. Back to work under the eyes of Coudrier's walking cameras. Wherever I went in the damn place, I could feel them watching me. But I couldn't see them. All very pleasant. I spent my time furtively glancing around left, right and centre. Sod all. The two of them obviously knew their job well. During that day, I sent customers flying on ten occasions when looking behind my back. Moans started and I picked up their scattered packages. Then: "Monsieur Malaussène is requested at the Customer Complaints Office." So Monsieur Malaussène went. Monsieur Malaussène did his job, while waiting rather impatiently to be fired: on the day Aunt Julia's article came out, which was now running late. On my way back down from Lehmann's office, I dropped into the book department and picked up a copy of the *Life of Aleister Crowley*, identical to the one I'd torn to shreds. Old Risson took my money after making a long, disapproving sermon. I completely agreed with him. My poor Thérèse, this certainly wasn't literature, but never mind, I was still going to repair the damage I'd done. I was even going to ask Theo to bring round another Yemanja.

(I could hear Julia's laughter: "You will never possess anything completely, Benjamin Malaussène, not even your own anger." Then, later that night: "So it now looks like I want you, too. To be my aircraft-carrier, Benjamin. Will you be my aircraft-carrier? I'll come and land on you from time to time so that you can fill me up." Touch down, my lovely, then take off as often as you want. From now on I'll be sailing in your coastal waters.)

But Chief Superintendent Coudrier's invisible cameras weren't the only things eyeing me up. The entire Store was gawping at my rainbow-coloured face. Which made one hell of a lot of eyes. I couldn't see Cazeneuve. Was his sick leave longer than mine? That kick in the nuts I gave him! It must have sent his sperm spurting out his lug-holes. Sorry, Cazeneuve. Really I am. (Julia's laughter again in my mind: "From now on I'm going to call you *the other cheek*.") So where were those two coppers hiding? "Monsieur Malaussène is requested at the Customer Complaints Office . . ." So I went . . . So I went . . .

After which, I thought I'd drop in on Miss Hamilton, just to see how my turn-on factor was functioning now that I really knew Aunt Julia.

In Lehmann's office, a woman was screaming. A deodorant spray had turned into a grenade in her delicate hand, swelling it up into a boxing glove. Lehmann did a good routine on my "criminal negligence". But the customer just wouldn't withdraw her complaint. She even looked bent on driving her stiletto heels into my tearful cauliflower of a face . . . (That's life, Lehmann my old mate. You can't win 'em all.)

So, after the bollocking, I popped in to say "hi" to Miss Hamilton. All I wanted to know was whether her curves still made me go perpendicular, or whether Julia was now fully established as the biblical knowledge of my life. I clambered up the stairs and said: "Hi, there, it's me!" Miss Hamilton had her back to me, engrossed in daubing her nails with some varnish which was as transparent as her voice. One of her hands, raised up in the light, revealed its nail-cloud. But all varnishes smell the same, I needed just the swiftest glance at that little mechanical beauty to be certain that she was no Julia. All the same, I cleared my throat. Miss Hamilton turned round. Jesus Christ! Jesus fucking Christ! She looked just the same as I did! Her make-up tried but failed to conceal two whopping black eyes, which almost closed her lids. Her upper lip was split and so swollen that it almost blocked her nose! Fuck me. Who on earth had done that to her? The answer immediately span round my head, like a coin on a plate. The inevitable piling up of evidence that you are powerless to resist. It was you, fuck-face, it was you who did that to her! The woman's body on the pavement had been hers! She was the one you thumped!

It took me a good while not to get over this. Who'd laid the spiel on her? Malaussène "a basic explanation", Malaussène "a patent cause", Malaussène the Bombergoat. Who? Cazeneuve? Lecyfre? And why had she believed them? And me, reckoning she had a soft spot for me! How perspicacious of you, Malaussène! Congratulations! As plonkers go, you really are a king-size. It was all your fault! You and your lousy fucking job! You and your goat stench!

Miss Hamilton and I stared at each other for a moment, just like that, both struck dumb, then two little tears flowed down the ruin I'd made of her face, and I scarpered like a traitor after the night of the long knives.

I was up to here with it. I was up to here with it, here with it, here with it. (I was pretty much up to here with it . . .)

Stojil! I was in a state of mind where I badly needed Stojil's company. Because disillusions were something Stojilkovitch had been through from A to Z. First of all there had been God, who he'd firmly believed in but who had then slipped away from him, leaving him exposed to the four winds of History. Then the heroism of war, and its absurd symmetry. Next came the smug fattening up of the Comrades, once the revolution had been won. Last of all came the leper's solitude of exclusion. Everything had been ballsed up during the course of his long life. What was left? Mating (at chess) and even there he did lose sometimes. What else? Humour. Humour, that last-ditch ethical expression.

So I spent part of the night with Stojil. But no way was I going to shove wood about. I needed him to talk to me too much.

"All right, my lad. As you see fit."

With his hand on my shoulder, he took me on a guided tour of the entire Store. He dragged me along from one floor to the next and, in his beautiful subterranean voice, spoke to me about every least article (a pressure-cooker, tinned cassoulet, baby-doll nightdresses, escalators, Pléiade Classics, lampstands, paper flowers, Persian rugs) in his historico-mystical tone, as though it were a compact monument to our civilization being visited by two wise Martians.

After that, we laid out our pieces on the chessboard. Just couldn't resist it. But this was going to be a fun game, a chatty game, during which Stojil would press on with his inspired basso-profondo monologue. Until we got (God knows how) to Kolia, that young German-killer who'd gone mad at the end of the war.

"As I told you, he really had worked out umpteen ways to kill. There was the one with the pregnant accomplice and the pram, of course, but he also got himself into bed with a few officers. (The S.A. Brownshirts weren't the only Nazis to adore angelic faces.) Or else he created accidents, scaffolding collapsed, a car wheel came off, that sort of thing. When he was behind it, Death most often looked like a coincidence, an accident, a stroke of bad luck. Two of the officers with whom he openly went to bed (a sort of Balkan Lorenzaccio, do you see?) died of heart attacks. Not a trace of poison was found, not a sign of violence. Other officers then protected him from the Gestapo. Nearly all of them desired him and hence they were fostering their own deaths. They must have vaguely suspected this, because they used to jokingly call him 'Leidenschaftsgefahr'."

"Which means?"

"'The dangers of passion', all very German as you can see, very Heidelberg! And, little by little he became the incarnation of the Angel of Death. Even for our people, who now found it difficult to look him in the eye. I suppose that this, too, contributed to his madness."

The incarnation of death. That little photo flashed into my mind. Leonard's tense muscles, his pointed, gleaming skull, the legs of that dead child . . . it was then that I asked him:

"Did he ever use explosives?"

"He did use bombs sometimes. The great maximalist tradition."

"So he killed innocent passers-by, then?"

"Never. That was his obsession. He devised a directional-bomb technique, which the Russian and American secret services were later to perfect."

"Directional bombs?"

"The idea is simple enough. You make as much din as you can while making the least possible amount of damage. A big noisy explosion to fire lead shot at a particular target."

"What's the point?"

"To make a premeditated murder look like a random terrorist attack. If there is an investigation, the first idea is that it was a coincidence. It could easily have been you or me or, given the din, ten other people. Kolia generally killed collaborators that way. Yugoslavs murdered in the middle of a crowd."

A pause, during which Stojil turned back to the game. Then, in his thoughtful chessplayer's voice:

"If you ask me, the character who's operating in the Store at the moment has adopted precisely the same strategy."

Chapter 25

LET'S JUST SUPPOSE. Let's suppose that our bomber really wasn't killing at random. His victims had been selected. The police misled into looking for a crazy killer. As far as they were concerned, pure luck alone had saved the customers from being slaughtered. What was more, the second bomb had killed two people instead of one. Right. So just imagine that the police were barking up the wrong tree after a hit-or-miss maniac. Despite the fact that their labs must have analysed the bombs. So just suppose that they hadn't come up with anything conclusive. Question time. If the killer knew his victims and was wiping them out one after the other: 1) Why always in the Store? Objection, he might well be killing others elsewhere without you knowing anything about it. Possible, but not likely. Four victims in one place made that a pretty shaky hypothesis. 2) If the killer knew his victims and was wiping them out one after the other, did they know him, or one another? Probably. 3) But if these budding stiffs knew each other, why did they insist on doing their shopping in the Store? I reckon I'd avoid the place like the plague if three of my mates had been blown away there. Conclusion: the victims didn't know each other, but the killer knew them all individually. (A lad who had the knack of making friends at every level of society.) Right. So, back again to the first question: Why did he always top them on the Store's premises? Why not at home in bed, at a red light, or in their local hairdresser's? No answer to that question for the moment. So straight on to question number 4: How the hell did he manage to get his bombs into the Store, given the fact the coppers frisked everyone during the day and patrolled the place at night? Not to mention Sentryman Stojilkovitch. Any answers? None. All right, so question 5: WHY THE FUCK WAS I UP TO MY EARS IN IT? Because there were no two ways about it, every time something went pop, there I was. And, each time, I emerged unscathed. Upon which, an attack of cold sweats, the elimination of questions 1, 2 and 3 and the return to Chief Superintendent Coudrier's working hypothesis. The killer didn't know any of his victims. I was the one he had it in for and no-one else. He wanted to drop me as deeply as possible in it. So, he spent his time following me around and, whenever the time seemed ripe, "bang!", he blew up someone standing next to me. But if he had it in for me so much that he wanted to frame me up for this terrible business, why didn't he just TNT me and be done with it? That would be even nastier, wouldn't it? And anyway, if all of that was true, then who the hell was he? My memory became a gaping black hole. I just couldn't see who. Then back once more to question 1: Why was he setting me up only *inside* the Store? Why didn't people start dropping dead in the street when they passed me, why didn't they blow up in the métro when they sat down opposite me? No, it had to be linked to the Store. But if everything depended on my presence in the Store, all I'd have to do was leave and then the slaughter would stop, wouldn't it? Question 6 cropped up: Why was Chief Superintendent Coudrier giving me so much rope? Just so that he could trap a crook who was as crafty as he was himself? Quite likely. He was quiet and dogged, was old Coudrier. This was a challenge for him, and one that he'd accepted. Specially since it wasn't his arse that was on the line. A little ball-game was going on between top-level goodies and baddies. Right now, the baddy was leading four–nil.

These were the sort of questions which were racing through Benjamin Marlowe's or Sherlock Malaussène's brains, while he absentmindedly let his kegs fall down round his ankles. Despite the stench of Julius the Lolling Tongue, Aunt Julia's scent could still be made out in my bedroom. ("You've really got the family spirit stamped on your soul, Benjamin; you've been in love with your little sister Clara ever since she was born, but as you are too moral to be incestuous, you make love with another woman, who you call your aunt.") Her scent wafted through the room. I smiled. ("What would the world come to if you weren't there to explain it, Aunt Julia?") Julius's eye followed the stages of my solitary striptease. He was lying at the foot of my bed. He no longer welcomed me home by flattening me. He no longer leapt up at the mention of a walk. He sniffed at his grub before gulping it down. He looked at everything he saw with profound worldly wisdom. He'd met Dostoevsky in Epilepsy Land and Fyodor Mihailovich had explained everything to him. Since then, old Julius had been acting mature. It was really weird. Specially because his stuck-out tongue made him look like a permanent schoolboy. And didn't he stink! Maybe I could make the most of his new-found wisdom and teach him to wash himself . . .

"Good idea, Julius. What do you reckon?"

He raised a pink eye at me, in which I could read that the summit of doggy wisdom consists in *never* having a wash.

"As you like . . ."

Lights out. It'd been a knackering day, in fact. But it still had one more surprise in store for me before I could hit the hay. When pulling back my bedcover, I found a sheet of paper covered with some constipated lettering under my pillow. Great. So what sort of surprise was it? A declaration of love, or of war? I picked it up between my thumb and index finger, put it under the bedside lamp and discovered it was in Thérèse's handwriting. She hadn't spoken to me since my religious fury. It was a Sergeant-Major's hand, with perfect curls, absolutely impersonal, as if she'd learnt it off some mid-nineteenth century schoolmistress. A moment's worry. Then a smile. Thérèse was out to make peace. With a tinge of humour I found odd coming from her. She was giving me her predictions for the next big race. Clara'd obviously taken me literally.

My dear Ben,
It will be the 28, the 3, the 11, or the 7, with a high probability for the 28.

Your affectionate sister,
Thérèse xxxxx

OK, so I decided to gamble on my dear sister Thérèse's numbers the next day. If Clara managed to sell her photos and Thérèse came up with one lottery win per year, then I could put my feet up on a private income . . . (In fact, my sole ambition was to turn my family into earners. I wasn't sacrificing myself, I was making an investment.)

After that, I dozed off. But it was only to wake up again at once. That insidious round of questions, lurking at first, then increasingly present, lit up all my neurons. My head became clear. I thought again about that photo which was stashed in the drawer of my bedside table. But not, this time, in terms of its horror. No, but as a clue. Our only clue. And one that Theo wanted to keep back from the police. I didn't want to go behind my mate's back, but I was definitely going to have to explain to him that we were playing with dynamite. How long did you get for concealing evidence? Wasting police time? Perhaps even aiding and abetting? Theo, Theo, you were going to have to give the cops that photo, if you didn't want to have the two of us sent down. I loved my adored city's carbon monoxide and lead-poisoning. I didn't want to be deprived of them. So, why the hell had I kept that photo, then? So that Theo wouldn't run any risks being caught on his way home? Not really. I'd kept it so that I could study it more closely. I'd sniffed out something. Thanks to my infallible intuition. The sort of superb intuition which had made me sure Miss Hamilton fancied me. (Mamma mia . . .) So I took the photo out of its drawer and had a close look at it. I hadn't noticed that the child's right foot had been cut off, and was being held in Leonard's left hand! And what on earth could that heap be, by the table leg? A pile of clothes? No,

Theo. It was something else. But what? No idea. What about the background darkness? Here and there, it looked like it was haunted by deeper shadows. Jesus Christ, all that darkness . . . and that gleam of mutilated flesh!

Chapter 26

HANDS CLASPED ON their firearms, the members of the flying squad leapt into their armour-plated trucks. Doors could be heard slamming, then the long wail of a siren, followed by the flashing of lights beaming out from the gaping garages. Standing up on their stirrups, the motorcyclists were already opening the way, sticking out their round buttocks like charging cavalrymen. Paris faded away in front of them. Panicked cars clambered up onto the pavements and pedestrians leapt up onto benches. Three fire stations released their red monsters, whose painted chrome was even shriller than the sirens. There was also the long, pale cry from the ambulances, and the choppers slicing their way through the saturated atmosphere of the capital. The fat round Television Centre let loose its pack as well, film units and cars bristling with aerials. Soon they were followed by their colleagues from the press in their company cars and by the independent radioheads on their personal mopeds. All of them were heading south, worked up into a paroxysm of professional excitement. On Place d'Italie, an armoured car shot out from Boulevard de l'Hôpital and barged straight into a fire-engine, which was turning out from Les Gobelins. Blue versus Red. There was no winner. Just an equal number of helmets on the tarmac. An ambulance swept them up, then headed back to where it had come from.

On the south-bound autoroute this screaming convoy acted like a pump, sucking up in its wake an armada of passers-by, that huge and healthy crowd of bloodthirsty on-lookers who started hooting their horns as well, as though they were out celebrating the New Year. They had to drive for seventeen kilometres, which they covered in one shallow breath, in a twinkling of an eye. The air was so pent with urgency, that they didn't even have the time to wonder where they were going before they'd arrived. SAVIGNY-SUR-ORGE. That was where it was all happening. Or, to be more precise, it was in that cute rose-covered house on the bank of the Yvette. Its shutters down, surrounded by emptiness, with an odour of death. And a watchful silence. One of those silences through which a line of sharpshooters goes running, here ducking behind a car, there climbing onto an old tiled roof, or else lurking behind the canvas sides of a truck, each and all of them in touch with their chief via walkie-talkie, fingers on the triggers of their telescopic-sighted rifles, not so much men as looks and bullets. The TV commentator, who'd kept up a football match patter until then, suddenly started whispering, whispering how it was here, inside that cute house with its flower-filled windowboxes, that the Store Bomber was holed up, and that he had, apparently, taken his old father hostage. The house was crammed with explosives, enough to blow the entire village to kingdom come, so they had evacuated the area within a three-hundred-yard radius.

Silence in the Store, where the image of that charming house had flickered onto a good hundred colour screens. Staff and clientele alike stood there together, struck dumb, eyes staring, in the television display room. Its four walls, tessellated with the same image, promised an end worth waiting for. The time was then 20.18. It had all started at 20.00 hours. The police had decided to operate live, during the TV news bulletin on all channels, all of whom had been warned before operations began. The suspect had, in fact, been suspected for some time. So why hadn't he already been arrested? the whispering commentator pondered. Then answered his question himself: the building-up of evidence, until it all came together into such a watertight case that this assault became justified. Now, the suspect's resistance was as good as an open confession. In any case, he had screamed out his guilt in front of everyone, before barricading himself inside. He'd sworn to blow the house up at the slightest attempt to take it by storm. So everyone was waiting. Waiting. Especially one man, one lonely man who bore the entire responsibility for the mission. The camera then momentarily left that little house's flowery façade, to glide across no-man's-land and pin him down, him, the Man in Waiting. He was short and dressed in a dark-green coat. His jacket was a little too large for him, so that it looked like a sort of riding-coat. He was wearing the Légion d'Honneur and his pot belly filled out his silk waistcoat, which was embroidered with golden bees. One of his hands, stuck between two of his waistcoat buttons, was resting on his stomach, which was presumably riddled with the ulcers of responsibility. The other was hidden behind his back, perhaps to conceal the tenseness of his fingers.

His underlings stood at a respectful distance. He wasn't the sort of leader whose meditations could be disturbed lightly. His head lowered, as though bowed under the weight of his thoughts, a dark stare emerged from under his arched eyebrows, which was obviously aimed at that flower-girt house. A heavy black lock of hair, shaped like a comma, punctuated his broad white forehead.

So what was Chief Superintendent Coudrier waiting for, before giving orders for the final assault? He was waiting. Knowing from experience that haste loses battles. Knowing, too, that all his past successes, his career, not to mention his fame, were due to his innate ability to seize the right moment. Precisely the right moment. That was his sole and unique secret. So, he waited. Under the stare of the cameras, in the watchful silence of his underlings, in front of that house with the flowers, he waited. He had been handed a megaphone, but he'd waved it away. He wasn't a man for negotiations. Just for waiting. Then the lightning move. Suddenly, there was a disturbance behind the Great Man's back. But he didn't turn round. A dented pink 504 convertible, with six cylinders, as lethal as a pike, broke through the crowd of journalists and policemen. With a sigh, it pulled up beside the Great Man. Two men leapt out of it, without even touching the doors, which remained locked. Two cat-like bounds. As they walked towards their boss, the camera caught their faces. The smaller one had the tormented ugliness of a hyena. The other was a massive bald man, hairless except for the sideburns that dotted their exclamation marks onto his powerful jaws. The former was dressed like a tramp, the latter like a golfer.

"Harry Hyena and Sid Burns!"

"Spot on, kids."

"Meaner than Phil Coffin and more bent than the Bouncing Czech!"

"In the flesh, Jeremy. You recognised them."

"So?"

"So what?"

"So what happens next?"

"What happens next will be at the same time tomorrow."

"Shit, no, Ben! Don't be such a mean fucker!"

"Sorry?"

"I mean, go on, you can't leave us in suspense like this!"

"Do you want me to take a look through your school exercise books, just to see how much of a mean fucker I can be?"

(Ah! . . . Pause for thought.)

Then Jeremy turned towards Clara (the way he got his five-year-old's smile back when he really needed it was quite something!)

"Clara, you tell him . . ."

Then Clara's voice:

"Go on, Ben . . ."

That was all I needed for my authority's last pocket of resistance to collapse.

So the shorter and uglier of the two inspectors (it was impossible to say which one was nastier) leant over the Great Man's ear. There was a whispering, then the shadow of a smile flickered over the leader's face. And in that shadow, all the observers could read that victory was now certain. All Chief Superintendent Coudrier had to do was raise his hand and snap his fingers for his faithful Inspector Caregga to appear, like a loyal jack-in-the-box.

For a second, the TV screens clouded over. Then, the commentator's talking head appeared once more. He was explaining that the siege of the house was likely to be a long one, so he suggested that the viewers might like to listen to Doctor Pelletier, the world-famous psychiatrist, who was going to try to analyse the personality of the bomber for us. The commentator turned round towards his guest, whose face then filled up the screen. Every young lady in France immediately trembled with emotion, as did their mothers. For Professor Pelletier was extremely young – unless, that is, he was a man kept youthful by his intelligence – with pale, fragile good looks, who spoke in a calm, soft voice which was so deep that it made him sound like night watchman Stojilkovitch. He began by paying homage to the criminal's exceptional intelligence. Nobody before, in the annals of crime, had ever given the police the run-around for so long, while committing the same crime in the same place, using the same means, on so many different occasions. Doctor Pelletier then smiled sweetly, so sweetly that everyone forgot that he was talking about a dangerous killer. "And," he went on, "in this case, his intelligence comes as no surprise to me. For I knew the man in question for many years during my childhood, we went to the same school together and I never managed to beat him to first place. We used to compete ferociously against each other, as children do at school, and in many respects it is thanks to my emulation of him that I have reached the position I am now in today. So, please don't expect me to make any moral judgment of my old friend. I shall simply try, to the best of my ability (though I'm quite sure that, still today, he could do a better job of it than I) to explain what lies behind his apparently mindless acts."

"Another cup of coffee, please, Clara."

Jeremy and Half Pint started yelling:

"Later, Ben. What happens next? Please, what happens next?"

"I've got time for a quick coffee break, haven't I? You're not paying me by the hour, you know. Anyway, it's almost finished . . ."

"Finished? What do you mean 'finished'?"

"What do you think happens at the end?"

"They blow the place up with a bazooka!"

"Good idea. And, with all those explosives inside, Savigny gets wiped off the map. Well done, the boys in blue!"

"They get in through the sewers."

"Half Pint, you can't use the sewer trick several times in the same story. That'd be boring."

"How then, Ben? Finish your coffee for crying out loud!"

"What happened was exactly what Sid Burns and Harry Hyena had dreamed up in their sick imaginations. This criminal, this bomber, wasn't really as smart as Professor Pelletier was cracking him up to be. OK, he was far from being as thick as a docker's sandwich, but he hadn't exactly invented sliced bread either. So, when he heard our shrink sketching out this loving portrait of him on the box, he obviously left the window where he'd been watching to get a good look at the set. (From the flickering blue light behind the shutters, Harry Hyena had sussed that he was following his own epic adventures on the idiot box.) And when Professor Pelletier (who was no more a psychiatrist than I am, by the way, but had been good mates with our two coppers since the days of their wild youth), so, when this pseudo trick-cyclist started saying how they'd been school pals, how much he'd admired him and so on, chummy started scratching his bonce and wondering 1) what year that had been in, and 2) how he'd managed to forget such a good mate. These were, my children, two fatal questions, because he was still trying to answer them when he felt Sid Burns's ·38 nuzzle into the nape of his neck. I reckon at that very moment he already had Harry Hyena's cuffs round his wrists."

"But how did the two of them get into the house?"

"Through the front door. With their skeleton key."

Silence as always at this point in the tale. A slightly worrying silence, during which I could see the kids' synapses flashing away behind their motionless eyes and below their creased foreheads. They were looking for the weak link, some narrative ploy (a deceptive short cut, some wool over their eyes, a piece of sleight of hand) which was unworthy of my talents and of their perspicacity.

"It hangs together, Ben. In fact, that was dead smart of Sid Burns and Harry Hyena."

Phew!

"But what about his dad?"

Ah!

"No more a hostage than you or me. In fact, it was because of him that his son was booby-trapping the store."

"Really?"

The three of them jumped up again. Only Thérèse quietly continued her humble stenography.

"The father was an inventor and he claimed that the Store's three main suppliers had stolen his inventions. Which wasn't completely wrong, but not completely right either."

"What do you mean?"

A moment of narrative delight . . . "Well, he was the sort of bloke that never struck it lucky. He really had made all sorts of brilliant inventions (a pressure-cooker, a ball-point pen, you get the picture) but always two or three days after someone else had invented them. You can swallow that kind of thing once, maybe even twice, but if it keeps on happening, you wind up feeling like someone's got it in for you. So he finally managed to convince his son that the three firms were double-crossing him and his son decided to revenge him by booby-trapping the Store. Simple as that."

"What was the father doing when Harry Hyena and Sid Burns went into the house?"

"He was listening to friend Pelletier on the box as well! It has to be said that the father had never noticed that his son had been that brilliant at school. As a matter of fact, all he could remember was bawling him out on that score. So, obviously the father started listening too. He just couldn't believe his ears. He even apologized to his son. He'd been so unfair to him for so long! He apologized with tears in his eyes . . ."

Chapter 27

After my tale, it took us some time to bed the kids down. The flow of the story had set a mill of questions spinning. Among other things, Jeremy asked how the "criminal" (they adored this word, preferring it to "murderer") had managed to get the bombs inside the Store. That caught me napping. And Clara saved my skin by telling him that, for the moment, everybody was in the dark, but the "criminal" was about to be questioned by a young police inspector, a certain Jeremy Malaussène, who apparently had his theory about that.

"Too right," Jeremy murmured with a thoughtful grin, then slid down between his sheets without asking another thing.

When Julius and I got back to our bedroom, it was spotless. It hadn't been clean like that for donkey's years. Julius's stench was barely detectable and Julia's scent had vanished. Clara, who'd clambered up behind us, after claiming that she needed me to explain a Baudelaire sonnet, which she didn't understand very well, apologized with a smile.

"The housework hadn't been done for ages, Ben. So I made the most of some gaps in my timetable."

I immediately thought about that photo. The night before, I'd left it on my bedside table and, that morning, I'd forgotten to hide it away in the drawer. I glanced across. Of course it wasn't there any more. Then I glanced at Clara.

Tears were welling up in her eyes.

"I didn't do it on purpose, Ben."

(You fucking idiot, leaving it lying around like that . . .)

"I'm sorry, Ben. Honestly I am. I didn't mean to . . ."

There were no longer just tears in her eyes, she was now sobbing convulsively. I stupidly wondered to myself whether this was because of the horror she'd seen, or the shame at having been nosy.

"Ben, say something . . ."

Of course. I had to say something.

"Clara . . ."

There, I'd said something. How many years had it been since I'd last cried? (Mum's voice: "You never cried, Ben, in any case, I never saw you cry, even when you were a baby. Have you ever cried?" "No, mother dear, never, except when I'm working.")

"Ben . . ."

"Look, my Clarinette, it's all my fault. That photo should have been given straight to the police. Theo was the one who found it. He cried just like you when he showed it to me. But he didn't want them to arrest the person who avenged the dead child . . . Clara, are you listening to me?"

"Ben . . . I photographed it."

(Wonderful. Just perfect. But what did it matter? She'd seen it now, anyway . . .)

She sniffed another couple of times, then dried her tears.

I'd once asked her where this habit of photographing the most horrible things she ran into had come from (leaving aside her quite normal passion for photography). She told me that it was like when she'd been a little girl and I'd put something she didn't like onto her plate. "I never told you it was horrible, Ben, but the less I liked something – chicory for instance, with its bitter taste – the more I *tasted* it carefully. To *find out*, do you see? It didn't make me like it any more, of course, but as soon as I'd understood why I didn't like it, I managed to eat it without being fussy and irritating you. Well, it's a bit similar with photography. That's the best explanation I can give you."

So now Clara had photographed it, had she *found out*? And what the hell could you have found out, my poor darling?

"Clara, you should never have seen that thing . . ."

"Yes, I should. If I can be of any help."

The tone of her voice had just changed. That sweet precision was back.

"I made a few blow-ups."

(Christ . . .)

"In some of them, I've toned down the contrasts, in others I've heightened them."

(Good. Let's talk technical.)

"And three things seem odd. Do you want to see?"

"Of course I want to see!"

(I was not going to leave her all alone in that black-and-white world.)

Two seconds later, a dozen blow-ups were spread out over my bed. Bits of shadow, table legs, the heap on the floor, some of the images were increasingly white, while others were increasingly dark. The most remarkable thing was that they didn't contain a single scrap of the two bodies! As if they'd never been in the photo. Totally spirited away! What made this all the more striking was that Clara's eye had obviously grasped the *whole thing*, and not just the child and the murderer. And so an angel's eyes had obliterated that horror of horrors. Almost as if she was setting me a riddle, Clara playfully asked:

"What do you think that form by the table leg is?"

"Theo and I were wondering just the same thing."

"Take a good look. Doesn't it remind you of anything?"

"Clara, for Christ's sake, what do you expect it to remind me of?"

"Look . . ."

She took a red felt-tip pen out of her bag and, like a child, carefully traced round the edge of that dense mass of shadow where it met the darkness of the surrounding room. As she did so, a shape emerged. Sharp points and bumps linked together by a contour. And the further the contour closed round onto itself, the more the shape started to make sense and look, in fact, familiar. Here was a pot belly, and there a stiffened neck, then pointed ears, a gaping mouth with a tongue sticking out that was reminiscent of Picasso's *Guernica*, the vague shape of a paw. It was the outline of a dog!

"Julius? . . . Julius!"

Cymbals clashed in my space-time continuum.

"How on earth did Julius get into that photo?"

"It isn't Julius, of course. It's another dog, Ben, *but in exactly the same state Julius was in when he was paralysed*!"

My little sister was now starting to sound like a coked-up Sherlock Holmes.

"And that, Ben, leads us to another observation!"

"Observe away, my darling, observe away."

"The scene in the photograph took place *inside* the Store, on the very spot where Julius had his fit."

"What makes you say that?"

"When Julius passed by there, he must have sensed something . . ."

"You're kidding, this photo must be at least twenty years old!"

"Forty, Ben. It comes from the 1940s. They gave up the deckle edges in the 1950s. Which is something we could confirm by making a test on the decomposition of its chemical components . . ."

Goodness me! My favourite little sister was turning into a forensic lab!

"But something puzzles me . . ."

"What?"

"It wasn't the first time Julius went to fetch you from the Store after your game of chess."

"No, it wasn't. Why?"

"Why did he only have a fit on that particular night?"

In my mind's eye, I glimpsed that bushy-eyebrowed bastard barring the canteen door and telling me to go down the escalator.

"Because we usually take a different route. It was the first time he'd gone that way."

"And it happened just in front of the toy department, didn't it?"

Which made me stare at her like she was starting to give me the creeps.

"How do you know that? I never told you!"

"Look."

Her red pen sketched another outline across a whitened blow-up. What emerged immediately was a muscular form that rose up, slightly askew, as high as the ceiling. Two more strokes and the folds of a hood appeared, then the fluffy outline of a beard. It was one of those stucco Father Xmases which had, for more than a hundred years, been tirelessly propping up the rest of the Store above the toy department.

"They're the only ones in the Store, Ben."

(A blow-up, a photo that spills the beans . . .)

"Is that all, Clara?"

"No. Leonard wasn't alone."

"There was at least the person who photographed him."

"Him and a few others."

Three or four of them according to the next path which her little pen took through the sombre depths of that old photo. And perhaps more of them, out of shot.

"OK, my darling. That's enough for today. Hide all of this away safely somewhere and, tomorrow, I'll give the original back to Theo so that he can hand it over to the police."

Chapter 28

"OVER MY DEAD body!"

This came out so violently and, even though he was trying his best to contain himself, with such a loud crash of his fork onto his plate, that the nearby customers jumped out of their skins and turned round.

"What's got into you, Theo? Look, you've just broken your plate."

"Just leave it out, Ben. There's no way I'm giving that photo to the police."

The grated celeriac and its dressing spread like running plaster of Paris over the red chequered tablecloth.

"You realize the risk we're taking?"

He discreetly tried to stick the two halves of his plate back together again. And sure enough, between the plate and tablecloth the celeriac made for a passable cement.

"You're not risking anything at all. All you have to do is chuck Clara's blow-ups away, then you're laughing. As for me . . ."

He glanced up rapidly.

"That's my business."

He spat the phrase out from between his teeth, in a ferocious whisper, as he was putting that sinister photo back into his wallet. It was now my turn to look at him quizzically, before asking him the same question he'd asked me the other evening:

"Theo, are you involved in this bombing business?"

"If I was, then I wouldn't have shown you the photo."

His reply was spontaneous and rang true. If he had had something to do with it, then he wouldn't have tried to get me involved by dangling a clue under my nose.

"Do you know who is, then? Are you covering for someone?"

"If I knew who it was, then I'd nominate him for the Légion d'Honneur. Bastien! Bring us another plate, will you? I've busted mine."

Bastien, our in-house waiter, giggled as he bent down over us.

"A lovers' tiff?"

For the last few months the jerk had assumed that we were a couple.

"Keep your witticisms to yourself and bring me back something more solid. And without grated celeriac! Which one of us Frogs invented grated celeriac, for Christ's sake, can you tell me that?"

Bastien crossly wiped down his bespittled face.

"No-one made you order it!"

"It was from sheer curiosity! The taste for adventure! There are times in your life when you want to be able to believe your own eyes, aren't there?"

All of which was spoken in a tone of persistent nastiness.

"Are there, or aren't there? Oh, get me a leek vinaigrette instead."

Focus on Bastien's fat arse as it waddled off cursing.

"Theo, why won't you give that photo to the cops?"

All his aggressiveness turned towards me. He looked like he was about to tell me where to stick myself.

"Do you ever read the newspapers?"

"The last one I read had Leonard's death splattered all over the front page."

"Did it? Then you had quite a stroke of luck. You must have got a copy of the first edition. The second was seized."

"Seized? Why?"

"By the deceased's family. Intrusion of privacy. The right phone call to the right place and within two hours every copy on sale had been hauled in. After that, they sued the rag's editor, slapped a writ on him, and they won their case this morning."

"That quickly?"

"That quickly."

Fat Bastien slithered over. The leek vinaigrette arrived on the table.

"But all that doesn't explain why you want to keep the photo."

He looked sorry for me.

"You got grated celeriac for brains, or what, Ben? You realize how powerful those squeaky-clean arseholes are? All they had to do was make one phone call to seize every copy of the newspaper which had dared print the four photos of that old bugger tossing himself off! (Because you have at least worked out what those photos were of, haven't you?) A case then goes like lightning through the courts and the rag has to cough up a pile of dosh. So what do you reckon will happen if I hand this photo over to the police?"

"They'll hush it up."

"Word will come down from on high. You're not as thick as I thought. So, do you want me to tell you what will happen?"

He suddenly leant forwards over his plate, and his tie plunged into it.

"This is what will happen: with this magnificent clue in their clutches, the coppers suss out the main point, i.e. the motive. So far they've been on a wild goose chase after a crazy, random killer. But now, they know. They know that a gang of shit-head Satanists used to celebrate – and maybe still does! – black fucking masses with human sacrifice, and all the physical torture that implies, on *children*, my good sir, on *children*!"

He was now on his feet, his fists on the table, his tie rising from his plate and climbing up to his neck, like a fakir's rope, with him looking as if he ought to be yelling his head off, but whispering, whispering, with tears quivering once more on his eyelashes.

"Your tie, Theo. Look at your tie. Sit down . . ."

"The penny drops. The pigs cop onto the rest. Someone's after our sacrificial fuck-faces and is bumping them off, methodically, one after the other, and this someone will nobble the lot of them if the pigs just stay sat on their arses. And the pigs wouldn't really mind this avenger doing the dirty work for them, but the Force is a public body and, as such, it must function, you see? Now these pigs function just like you and me (well, not really like me), they're curious, Ben, as curious as hell. They'd give ten years of their pensions to nick one, just one, of those child eaters, and prod him around a bit to see what he was made of. And then, what do you suppose would happen to our surviving ogre?"

"He'd spend the rest of his life inside."

"Precisely."

He sat down again, took off his tie and folded it away carefully.

"Precisely, in a deep, dark cell so that not a word leaked out. No trial. Follow me, sir, step inside, slam the door and throw away the key. Because, my good sir, there's no way a scandal like that could be allowed to damage people with telephones as powerful as the Leonards'."

"What about the children's families?"

There then followed a long pause, during which Theo stared down at his leek vinaigrette, as if it was the least easily identifiable object he'd ever seen in his life. Then he said dreamily:

"Tell me, Ben, what do you think an orphan is?"

(Daddy's gone, mummy too . . . A sinister whispering started in my head.)

"All right, Theo, it's somebody no-one will miss."

"Yes, my good sir."

The stubborn way he was staring at that leek! . . .

"Yes, Ben. And an orphan is as gullible as hell. He's someone whose only desire is to find someone else, to get into cars when offered sweeties, and gentlemen like our gentlemen just adore orphans."

There was something inside him struggling not to think any further into what he'd told me. He'd become totally rigid. A vision of a man fighting against his own visions. His knife gingerly poked at his leek, as if it were a thing unnameable, only just dead, or not yet alive.

"When I say 'orphan', I'm being too specific. Let's just say 'abandoned'. Our beautiful society produces no end of abandoned children who no-one gives a toss about, including all the institutions that are supposed to take them in: little Arabs on the run from other massacres, little Asians cast off on their own, kids running away from home, or from homes, mushrooming over the pavements, just take what you fancy, sir . . . No, I'm not giving that photo to the police."

He paused long enough to turn his leek over. It had the consistency of a drowned man.

"What's more, I reckon that the coppers will be arresting our avenger soon enough. They're no fools, they've got their ways and means, they can't have stayed on the random killer trail for that long. The race is now to the swiftest. And Zorro's only got half a length's lead. Perhaps not even that much. I'm sure he won't have time to nobble the lot of them. So that's why I'm not going to help the police nick him. No way, I'm not."

Then, at last, after a final look down at that pallid thing lying in his plate, its green and white colours melting into its thick oily mother-of-pearl dressing, complete with motionless eyes of vinegar . . .

"Ben, let's get the hell out of here. That leek's just about done my head in."

Chapter 29

IT HAPPENED DURING the morning, just before Louna phoned. I'd come out of Lehmann's office and popped into the first-floor book department to check out one of those apparently insignificant details which speed up investigations and save pages.

All I wanted to do was ask Monsieur Risson how long he'd been slaving away at the Store.

"It will be forty-seven this year! Forty-seven years spent fighting to defend the world of books, my lad, while selling penny dreadfuls. But, thanks be to God, I have always managed to keep my Literature section open!"

Forty-seven years in the Store! I didn't ask him how old he'd been when he started. I went on browsing and flicking over pages to justify his pride. I glanced at the *The Death of Virgil*, then flirted with a hardback edition of *Manuscript Found at Saragossa*, before asking him:

"How many copies of the Gadda have you sold since it was reissued in paperback?"

"What, *That Awful Mess on Via Merulana*? None."

"Well now you have. I have a present to buy."

His handsome old face gave a severe, critical pout of approval.

"Yes, there's a real book for you. Better than that gibberish about Aleister Crowley!"

"That was a present, too. There's no accounting for taste."

"If you want my opinion, there's no accounting for lack of taste."

While he was giftwrapping my purchase (it seemed to take him an eternity), I got nearer to what was on my mind:

"Do you never take a holiday? I don't think I've ever seen the book department without you."

"Holidays are for your footloose generation, young fellow. As for me, I soldier slowly on and only close when the Store does."

It was a golden opportunity. So I grabbed it.

"And how many times has the Store closed in the last forty-seven years?"

"Three times. Once in 1942, once in 1954, when they added on the sixth floor, and once in 1968, during that ridiculous carry-on."

(May, '68, a "ridiculous carry-on"?)

"And what made it close in 1942?"

"How can I put it? There was a change of owners, of management and of policy. The previous board had mostly been Jews, if you see what I mean. But that was a period when we didn't hesitate to give true Frenchmen back what belonged to them!"

(What?)

"So how long did the Store remain closed?"

"For a good six months. You see, those 'gentlemen' tried to haggle over the price. But History was soon to settle their score. Thank God."

(If God exists, then he'll shit on you when the time's ripe, you old cunt.)

"Six months left empty?"

"But carefully guarded by the Militia to stop the rats from emptying the ship."

(Just to think that, until then, I'd always found this old shit-head wonderfully pleasant company, the grandfather I'd never had and all that sentimental crap . . .)

Reminding myself to disinfect it later, I snatched poor old Gadda from his hands and said:

"Thanks very much, Monsieur Risson. I'll come back for another chat whenever I have the chance."

"Please do. Respectful young men are a rare breed these days."

* * *

It hit me on the escalator. That sword of fire straight through the skull. Total pain. Spiced up with a grotesque vision from some Chester Himes book: a big Black, running through the New York night, with a knife stuck into one temple and coming out the other. Then, the pain calmed down and my deafness returned. No more rhubarb rhubarb, no more muzak, zilch. Too late. It hadn't stopped me hearing the granddad of my dreams talking about the good old days. Jesus fucking Christ. How could someone with such a huge pile of shit where his brains should be love Gadda, Broch, Potocki and agree with me about Aleister Crowley? When would I finally manage to understand something about anything? Still, I had discovered the date. 1942. If anything had gone on inside the Store, then it must have been during the six months of that year. During the day, or at night? At night, judging by the photo. At night. In a Store guarded by the Militia.

That's where I was at when I finally spotted them.

My two walking cameras.

Chief Superintendent Coudrier's peepers.

They suddenly stuck out like such a pair of sore thumbs that I wondered how I hadn't noticed them before. Little and Large. Fat and Skinny. Neat and Scruffy. Bald and Hairy. Sid Burns and Harry Hyena. Or nearly. With that inevitable gap that life puts between truth and fiction, no matter how hard you try. But still, why hadn't I spotted them before? A pair of gawks like that! The fat one was hiding behind the fancy leather goods counter, while, fifteen yards away, Mr Hyde was stuffing his face with a chocolate cream cake amid the lady's lingerie. I was so flabbergasted that I couldn't take my eyes off them. They realized at once that they'd been rumbled. And they looked just as surprised as I did. So we sized each other up for a bit, then the fat one suddenly went purple and gave me a rapid nod which I understood immediately. He was as bugged as a second-hand PC and as muscle-bound as an Atlas. So I shook myself and looked elsewhere. Straight between the two of them, to be exact, so as to avoid his mate who was pigging out on the chocolate cream cake. It was then that things got even more complicated. Right bang in front of me, at about ten yards behind them, was the weapons department. With its displays of shooters, its complete range of alarm guns, hunting knives, ultrasonic whistles, animal-traps and all that what-have-you which brings a gleam of delight into a hunter's eyes – the sort of person who really knows and loves the natural world! There happened to be one of them standing by the counter – one of those greenies done up in paramilitary gear. About fifty years old, with his two dangerously clean-looking teenage offspring. All three of them were discussing the merits of a pump-action shotgun with a bluish gleam, which they were passing back and forth, taking aim in a flash, sketching tiny curves in their piece of sky, then nodding their heads like the true connoisseurs they'd obviously been since the cradle. The salesman was all smiles and clearly in deep communion with them. He was so over the moon at having such hot-shot customers that he wasn't even keeping his eyes on the rest of his counter any more. And that's when I saw a hand plunge into a grey cardboard box then reappear holding a couple of cartridges, as cool as you like, without even trying to be subtle about it. The hand belonged to one of Theo's little oldsters, really little, this one, and extremely old and who, of course, I recognised, and who recognised me, and who (cross my heart and hope to die!) openly showed me the cartridges with a broad grin on his face, before shoving them into the left pocket of his grey smock. I'd already seen the same gesture three times before. The first time was with that black remote control box, while Cazeneuve was picking up the AMX 30, the second was with the vibrator . . . and the third time . . . no, the third time had been a twisting movement given to a copper tap . . .

I immediately glanced back at the two coppers, who were staring at me like I was the prince of plonkers for standing there gazing into the wild blue yonder. The small one raised an eyebrow and shrugged a shoulder. "What's up with you, mate? Off duty already?" That's what his gesture meant. I looked pointedly back at the weapons counter. They finally turned round. But the little old man had gone. I felt rather relieved.

* * *

Two minutes later, still as deaf as a post, I was back down in the deep waters of the basement cruising after Jiminy Cricket. Jiminy Cricket! That was him to a tee! He had exactly that sort of funny little face, with a pug-nose, smoothed out by ultra old-age into Jiminy Cricketude! My two coppers were patrolling some way off. I couldn't stop looking at them, as though my eyes were being magnetically attracted by their blatant professionalism.

And the faces they pulled every time our eyes met! Their haggard gobs looked absolute daggers.

And not a trace of Jiminy. For the first time, I realized just how many grey smocks there were down there. And all alike in their ancientness. Countless, identical and solitary. Modern-day oldsters having nothing to do with one another. Theo! I had to warn Theo that one of his protégés had made off with some ammo from the artillery counter! In the wallpaper section Theo was busy giving some advice to a woman, who was as massive as an opera singer. The lady's jowls were explaining what she desired and Theo's head was nodding away merrily. He was going to flog her enough paper to cover her flat ten times over!

So I headed off towards Theo, but I'd only got about half way when three simultaneous events stopped me in my tracks. First, I clearly spotted Jiminy, about ten yards away from me, emptying the powder from the cartridges into the metal head of a drill, with one eye on what he was up to and the other on me, a conspiratorial grin on his face, and impossible for the two coppers to single out, hidden as he was amidst half a dozen other identical little oldsters who were all hard at their DIY activities. Next came a heavy tap on my shoulder, which made a "plop" sound in my head, and finally Lecyfre's thunderous voice filled out the entire volume of my reopened skull:

"You in a trance, or what, Malaussène? They've been calling for you for the last five minutes! You're wanted on the phone. It's your sister. Apparently it's urgent."

* * *

"Ben?"

"Louna?"

"Ben! Oh, Ben!"

"What's the matter, Louna? What's wrong? Calm down now . . ."

"It's Jeremy."

"What do you mean, 'it's Jeremy'? Louna, my darling, try and calm down."

"He's had an accident at school. You've got to come at once. Ben . . . Oh, Ben! . . ."

Chapter 30

"IT IS A blessing that your brother was alone in the classroom."

("A blessing . . .")

The playground had become a steaming lake, scattered with the twisted wrecks of what manages to survive a fire. Long limp hosepipes snaked their way between the debris. An acrid smell of melted plastic hung around in the damp atmosphere. ("But the worst thing of all, between you and me, are first-degree burns . . . You just can't get rid of the stink . . . It stays in your hair for at least a fortnight.") That little fireman was a talking vision in my mind, while my nostrils were sniffing away, working hard to convince me that, amongst all those carbonized smells, there was not the smell of burnt flesh. Two jets of water finished hosing down the blackened shell. The three classrooms had been entirely gutted.

"Prefabricated buildings . . ."

One of those papier-mâché death-traps that go up at the slightest spark, that's what. Table legs and metal frames, going into meltdown, had flowed into one another and were now standing there fossilized into grotesque shapes. Held at a distance by the firemen, the pupils were alternating between feelings of grief, the desire to laugh and the still-fresh memory of being shit scared.

"Thank heavens that it happened during break."

("Thank heavens . . .")

One of the red trucks started reeling in its hosepipe. My mind's eye filled with the absurd image of a fork twisting up spaghetti.

"He'd gone off on his own . . ."

Spaghetti being slurped up along with a black octopus sauce. In which region of Italy did they eat that? . . .

"By the time we realized what was happening, it had already started to spread . . ."

"Why wasn't he outside during break like everyone else?"

"I have absolutely no idea."

"You have absolutely no idea?"

"I rather think that he was, I mean, that he is a highly independent child."

(He has absolutely no idea, he rather thinks, he means . . .)

"The fire started very rapidly . . ."

Yes, that's right. Rapidly. Like a match. A match that came very close to burning up a hundred kiddies. But it was "*a blessing*" that my Jeremy had been the only one left inside.

"It was a blessing, was it?"

"Sorry?"

"You said that it was 'a blessing', didn't you? And 'thank heavens'. . ."

"I beg your pardon?"

His eyes suddenly grew as big as his specs. I then realized that I was on my feet, leaning over him, while he was shrinking back into his chair.

Upon which, the phone rang. Without taking his eyes off me, he immediately answered it.

"Hello, yes? Yes, it is I."

("It is I" . . . "a blessing" . . . "thank heavens" . . .)

"At Saint-Louis Hospital, yes, in emergency admissions, yes I see, thank you awful . . ."

When he hung up again I was no longer in his office.

Laurent had got to Saint-Louis before me. When I arrived, he was in deep discussion with a bright-eyed, dark-haired little medic. As soon as I spotted them, I tried to read what was on their faces. All I could see was what can always be seen on professional faces when a pair of real pros get their heads together. The tall blond one and the short dark one, as thick as thieves from the word go. The brotherhood of know-all know-how. And the rest of it . . . I found the sight of them pretty reassuring, in fact. If Laurent was well in with this medic, then Jeremy was obviously in good hands.

"Ah! Ben, this is Doctor Marty." A touching of palms.

"Now, there's no call for alarm, Monsieur Malaussène. Your son's going to be fine."

"He isn't my son, he's my brother."

"That fact hardly alters his present condition."

This came out quite naturally, without a smile, with his eyes full on me. But, behind his specs, I could see an extremely comforting glint of jollity. I pulled together a make-shift smile and asked:

"Can I see him?"

"Only if you wipe that look off your face. I don't want you getting him down."

Funny bloke, this Marty. He said that in the same distantly jovial, cool-headed tone of voice, but something told me that if I didn't change expressions, then I wouldn't see Jeremy.

"Just tell me what's wrong with him . . ."

"Various burns, his right index finger severed and the fright of his life. But he has stubbornly refused to faint and has decided to play the comedian with the nurses."

"He's lost a finger?"

"We'll stick it back on in a jiffy."

Trust is a strange emotion. If Jeremy's head had just been blown off, I felt quite sure that this funny little fellow with his crisp delivery would simply stick it straight back onto his shoulders. He was efficiency made flesh. With something else as well . . . the human touch . . . "All right, is my face good enough for you now?"

He eyed me up and down for a moment, then turned to Laurent: "And what's your opinion, Bourdin?"

He was lying there naked. His body was covered with scabs which were crinkling up at the edges. His lips and right ear had swollen into chunks of a carnival mask. His head had been completely shaved. And when I went into his little disinfected room, the nurse who was sitting with him was in stitches. But, after a closer look, she was also crying at the same time. He was jabbering away, without moving an inch. His body was tiny. He was a real little boy, if you disregarded the volume of his natter.

He only noticed me when I was standing next to him. Then he smiled. The smile deteriorated into a painful wince. His face then seemed to stitch itself carefully back together again.

"Hi, Ben. Hey, I'm starting to look like Phil Coffin!"

The nurse looked up at me, her eyes full of sorrow and admiration.

"I've got something to tell you, Ben. In private."

And then, as if he'd known her for years:

"Marinette, you couldn't go and buy me a book, could you? You can read to me when this one here's gone."

I don't know if she was really called Marinette, but she obediently got to her feet and I went with her as far as the door.

"Don't tire him too much," she whispered. "They're going to take him down to the theatre in about ten minutes."

She added with a tender smile:

"I'll read to him while they give him the anaesthetic."

The door closed on the brightly lit corridor.

"OK, you alone now, Ben?"

"I'm alone."

"Come over here, then, and sit yourself down. I've got some important news."

I moved a chair up close to his bed. He waited for a moment, savouring the suspense. Then couldn't hold back any longer:

"I did it, Ben! I found out!"

"What did you find out, Jeremy?"

"How the 'criminal' got his bombs into the Store!"

(Jesus . . .) For a good long moment, all I could hear was his congested breathing and the beating of my own heart. Then I asked him:

"How?"

"He didn't take them in, *he made them on the inside*!"

(Sounds like I'd better take a seat after all.)

"No kidding?"

It cost me one hell of an effort to come out with that, and in such a jolly tone of voice.

"No kidding! I've tried it, and it works!"

"Tried it"? I knew we were now heading for the worst of it. The worst of it was approaching with its now familiar step.

"Ben, inside the Store there's everything you'd need to blow half of Paris to smithereens, if you felt like it."

True. But you'd still have to feel like it.

"At my school, too."

The ensuing silence was one hell of a silence.

"So, I did a little experiment."

"For Christ's sake, Jeremy, what 'experiment'? You're not going to tell me that you . . ."

"Made a bomb *during my lessons*, without anyone noticing."

(He was going to. And had.)

"You can use anything to hand, weedkiller, for example, for its sodium chlorate . . ."

And so it was that my little brother, who was merrily going on twelve, gave me a delicious recipe for a home-made bomb, getting more and more excited as his explanations went on, his voice merging with Theo's in my memory as he did so: "Just imagine it! One of them even spent all day walking round with five litres of weedkiller in his pockets!"

"Not so loud, Jeremy. And calm down, too. You mustn't tire yourself."

(What above all mustn't happen is for someone to hear him from the other side of the door, for crying out loud! My little brother, a child arsonist! And me, an educator, an upbringer . . .)

"It all went perfectly to plan, Ben, and then, just as I was defusing it, so as I could bring it home and show it to you, as a piece of 'incriminating evidence', see what I mean? Well, just then, the sodding thing blew up on me."

(And you burnt your fucking school down, for Christ's sake, Jeremy. YOU BURNT YOUR FUCKING SCHOOL DOWN!)

"Still, you do believe me, don't you?"

For the first time his voice was worried and trembling.

"Hey, Ben, say you believe me. Please!"

Silence. A long silence. I stared at him. More silence. And then tears started to roll across his singed eyelashes.

"You don't believe me, do you? I knew you wouldn't! Oh Ben, you know I've never lied to you . . ."

(Yahweh, Jesus, Buddha, Allah, Lenin, Thingamajig and Company . . . What have I ever done to you?)

"Of course I believe you, Jeremy. It'll be the last chapter of my story. This evening, I'll tell the others how the bombs were made in the Store. What a brilliant ending that will be! . . ."

Chapter 31

I live I perish I drown and I fry
I seethe with heat when suffering from frost
My life is far too smooth and yet too crossed
Great troubles all beside my joys do lie

"CLARA, WHEN YOU recite, you must respect the pauses. In poetry, silence plays the same role as it does in music. It is a moment's respiration. But it is also the shadow of the words, or their beaming out, as the case may be. Not to mention the silence of anticipation. There are many sorts of silence, Clara. For example, before you started reciting, you photographed that white cat on Victor Noir's tomb. Now, suppose we both remained silent after you finished reciting, would it then be the same silence?"

"Would it indeed, Benjamin, would it indeed? I wonder . . ."

She gently took the mickey out of me, while slipping her arm under mine. We continued our stroll through a sun-drenched Père-Lachaise, where Clara had just pointed out to me that practically all of the cats were either black or white. Or even black and white. But never coloured. I was thinking about Jeremy, whose finger had been stitched back on ten days before and who was due home the day after next. I was thinking about Julia, who'd been spending her nights trying to buck me up ("there's nothing the slightest bit *monstrous* about it, Benjamin, children are natural-born experimenters, which can certainly be a pain in the arse, but it isn't at all monstrous, and no, it isn't your fault, my little darling, so unwind, let yourself go, and don't make me start theorizing . . .") Julia, whose scent still protected me. I was thinking about that little old man, who I hadn't seen again in the Store, and who must have felt the coppers' eyes closing in on him.

And I was thinking about Clara, who had her French exam the next day and who didn't seem to understand a great deal about this Louise Labé sonnet.

"Louise Labé, sweetheart, let's get back to Louise Labé. Recite the second quatrain to me and try to mark the pauses. The examiner will give you extra marks if you do."

At the same instant I laugh and I cry
And in my pleasures am with torments tossed
My wealth is mine forever yet is lost
At the same time I blossom and turn dry

"So, what do you reckon she's on about, Clara? Why are all her nerves jangling, why the earthquake, why the short-circuits?"

"It sounds as if she's worried . . . worried, but very sure of herself all at the same time."

"Worried and certain. Yes, you're getting there. Now, recite the next line and stop there."

And so does Love inconstantly lead me

"Love, my Clarinette. It's Love that does that sort of thing to us. Look at your sister for instance."

At that, she stopped right in the middle of the pathway and photographed me.

"You're the one I'm looking at!"

Then:

"So who was this Louise? I mean, in relation to the other poets of her time, you know, Ronsard, Du Bellay and the rest?"

"She was the most accomplished character of the Renaissance. The subtlest poetry with the most revolutionary musical savagery. She was a swordswoman and used to disguise herself as a man so that she could take part in tournaments. At the siege of Perpignan, she even climbed the walls during the assault. After that, she honed her goose quill as fine as she could to write this, which is head and shoulders above all the other poetry of the period."

"Are there any portraits of her? Was she beautiful?"

"They called her 'La Belle Cordière'."

And so our stroll went on, with Clara taking photos and me unravelling that sublime sonnet for her, with her glancing at me with eyes full of wonder and me thinking, like Crosby's Cassidy, that if I was a teacher then I'd love the job for all the wrong reasons, one of which being my immoderate liking for this kind of naive admiration.

After Victor Noir's tomb, it was the turn of Oscar Wilde's mausoleum to get shot at. Theo wanted a blow-up of it for his bedroom. And thanks to Clara, he was going to get one.

Once Oscar Wilde was in the can, our walk was over, and it was time to fetch Half Pint from school. The last image on the way out was of three or four crones muttering muted incantations over the tomb of Allan Kardek. (Whose warts were they trying to cure, I wonder?) When Clara was on the point of immortalizing them, one of them turned round and waved at us to be off. Hissing like a cat, she scratched at the air.

It was at that precise moment that the fourth bomb exploded in the Store.

The fourth bomb . . .

During my day off!

It was an extremely simple home-made job: a dose of gunpowder rammed into a drill head + a small gas canister (as for camping) + . . . etc, set off at a distance by an ignition system borrowed from a television remote control.

A little bomb.

It peppered a sanitary equipment representative, of German origin, with shards of porcelain, while he was having a quiet piss in the bogs of the Swedish showroom on the top floor (lovely crappers, in fact, pure white and extremely hard-wearing – the door didn't blow – was so perfectly padded that no-one heard the bang – a discreet "pop" and that was that) while, then, the victim, a representative, was pissing.

And while gazing at a set of old photos he'd stuck up on the bog walls!

"Unfortunately" this one was a family man, the father of numerous offspring and a granddad many times over.

Probably a stamp collector into the bargain.

But he still wound up peppered with spotless porcelain. And scrap-iron. And buckshot, too.

And naked.

Naked?

As the day he was born. From tip to toe. Starkers, in fact.

Stripped by the explosion?

No, by himself, before it went off.

"But what we'd like to know, Monsieur Malaussène, is what your sister Thérèse was doing there, frozen like a statue in front of these Scandinavian water-closets, until we forced open the door and discovered the corpse. Yes, that's what we'd really like to know."

And so would I.

Chapter 32

"But, Ben, I did tell you so!"

She was standing there, as unbending as destiny, surrounded by three cops who looked fit for handing in their resignations. All around her, the fuzz were as busy as bees – if you can imagine bees typing reports while chain-smoking amid stacks of empty beer cans. So, there my sister Thérèse was, standing in the middle of the shabby office, with her elbows and knees jutting out, too tall for her age, in that stagnant fag smoke, with all those drones buzzing round her, all of which made my heart skip a beat.

"What did you tell me, sweetheart?"

Sid Burns's lookalike would have gobbled her down in one if he hadn't been frightened of breaking his teeth on her. The other one was fantasizing about another chocolate cake. Both of them looked like they'd had it.

"It's all we've managed to get out of her for the last hour!"

There was a third copper I didn't recognise, a young blondie, who was almost weeping with frustration.

"The only person I will speak to is my brother Benjamin. What's more, I did tell him."

"What did you tell him, for fuck's sake?" young blondie had yelled out in exasperation.

And, as he was extremely young, he had then added:

"Look, you little tart, you going come clean with us or what?"

In the end, they'd had to sit and wait for Caregga to show up, along with Suspect Number One, that is to say, my good self, who was now standing there in front of Thérèse and smiling fraternally at her, while other coppers were searching the flat, chucking everything all over the place in the ex-hardware shop and in my bedroom, filled with such a burning desire to find something (but what?) that they were just about ready to cut Julius in half and rummage around through his innards.

"Thérèse, what did you tell me?"

She started and looked at me like she'd just woken up.

"I told you that it would be the 28th, the 3rd, the 11th, or the 7th, *with a high probability for the 28th.*"

(Ah! So they weren't the numbers of horses, then . . .)

"I even wrote it down in black and white, in case you ever tried to contest my pronouncements."

("Contest my pronouncements". . . that sudden dig took me rather aback . . .)

"What is all this bullshit? You trying to bore us to death, or what?"

The blond kid was trying to make himself sound like a full grown hard-nut. The other two waited. Doors slammed. People were shouting at each other. A police station. My little Thérèse, we're in a police station!

"Thérèse, would you explain to these gentlemen what we are talking about?"

"You admit I was right?"

(That sounded like a "condition".)

"Yes, you were right Thérèse. I admit that."

"In that case, I'd only be too pleased to explain to these gentlemen . . ."

A little sentence which managed to freeze the entire office. Blondie sat himself down behind a typewriter. The ears belonging to the two pairs of peepers became imperceptibly larger.

"It's all very simple, gentlemen . . ."

She stood. They sat. The scenario had changed. She was now the Professor and they were the dunces trying to keep up with her.

"Extremely simple. Any one of you would have reached the same conclusions as I did. By dint of a little hard work."

Yes, that was how she started, in her shrill voice, sounding like she was giving a lesson at the Police Academy, entitled "Astrological Investigations into Murder."

She explained, with her thin bony head sticking up above the layers of fag smoke, breathing a faraway air as she always did, she explained to these "gentlemen" that the birth charts of the four previous victims had clearly shown that they would die violent deaths, on the very days they had died, not before, not after, and in that precise geographical location: the Store.

"So what day am I going to retire on?" the blond kid carped, unwittingly adopting Jeremy's role.

"Shut it, Vanini," Sid Burns's lookalike growled, taking a leaf from my book. "We've wasted enough time as it is."

"Forget about your little self and take down her statement, any old crap, even if it's a recipe for fruit cake. The boss will be along in a minute."

And Harry Hyena politely asked Thérèse to proceed.

"As for the fifth, potential victim," Thérèse went on, "given that I knew neither his name nor his age, I was not able to work forwards from his birth, but had to settle for a hypothetical point of arrival – what you call 'death' but which is, of course, nothing but a 'crossing-over' – then, once I had deduced a logical basis to work from, I tried to go back in time in order to discover the subject's point of emergence – what you call 'birth' but which is, of course, nothing but 'incarnation.'"

Chief Superintendent Coudrier's peepers were staring forwards like they could see straight through the wall, while the blond kid was typing away like a mad thing on a bloodless ribbon, which produced pale death-like letters. Thérèse was flying:

"So, bearing in mind the 'incarnation' dates of the previous four victims and the astral configurations which foretold their 'crossings-over' in the Store – or, if you prefer, their deaths – it seemed to me that the 28th day of this month, in the very same place, was the likeliest moment for a violent death, when Saturn was to cross over its own radical."

* * *

Thérèse had got herself up early that morning. She'd been the first customer into the Store. She'd trembled in horror during the frisky frisking she'd received from a sleepy-eyed policeman. She'd wandered through the still-deserted aisles, under the intrigued stare of the salesgirls who just couldn't believe that this girl with the Mystic Meg looks was really a shoplifter on the prowl. Then she'd mingled with the crowd as it delved into every nook and cranny in the Store, waiting for the moment when death would confirm her deductions, but also fearing that she was right, for my poor little Thérèse didn't want anyone to die "Ben, you believe me, don't you? You know I've never lied to you!" (that's right, exactly the same phrase that Jeremy came out with on his hospital bed) "I believe you, my darling, you wouldn't hurt a fly, I know that, now go on, we're all ears . . .", not knowing exactly where death would strike, but convinced by some dark illumination (the blond kid raised his eyes from his machine, but there was no doubt about it, "dark illumination" was definitely what she'd said) that, when the time was ripe, she'd know where and when.

And, when the time was well and truly ripe, they'd found a petrified young girl in front of the locked door of those double u c's which had come in from the cold. No-one had heard the explosion, the floor had in fact been practically empty at that low point of the evening – ten minutes before office closing time and the last rush of customers.

It was the head of department in person who'd discovered Thérèse. A big man with a high-pitched voice. Thinking that she couldn't make the bolt work properly, he tried to open the door for her. Locked from the inside. Intrigued, he waited there. But that silent, paralysed, gawky girl put the shits up him a bit. So he called for reinforcements. And the reinforcements brought along the police.

Who broke down the door.

On a peppered stiff.

With little photos on the blood-stained walls.

"And do you know what, Ben? I worked out his date of birth at the precise moment he died: December 19, 1922."

The blond cop's word machine-gun jammed with a metallic shriek. He glanced incredulously at the passport, which was lying open on the desk, and read out loud:

"Helmut Künz, German citizen, born in Idar Oberstein on December 19, 1922."

"I suppose you grasp how serious the situation has become, Monsieur Malaussène."

It was now far into the night. Caregga had taken Thérèse home. The station itself had nodded off. Only the rheostat in Chief Superintendent Coudrier's office indicated that the force was still with us. He was sitting behind his desk and I was standing in front of him. No Elisabeth. No cups of coffee. Nothing but one "educator" confronted by another "educator".

"Because the presumptions against you are beginning to mount up."

The light got slightly brighter to show how serious the moment was. (Chief Superintendent Coudrier created his lighting effects with a slight push of his foot onto a switch. Every copper must have his own little tricks.)

"And my men would not understand if I didn't take such things into account."

(Thérèse, Thérèse . . .)

"I shall now sum the situation up, if you do not have any objections."

(Don't bother on my account . . .)

But sum it up he did. In eight points, which tumbled out into the half-light like eight separate indictments:

1) Benjamin Malaussène, Quality Controller at the Store, a large business which has had bombs planted in it for the last seven months by an unknown killer, is always on the scene of each explosion.

2) When he isn't, then his sister Thérèse is.
3) The above-mentioned Thérèse Malaussène, a minor, seems to have predicted the time and place of the fourth explosion – something which might interest any police officer who remains sceptical about astro-logic.
4) Jeremy Malaussène, also a minor, burnt down his school by means of a home-made bomb, at least one of the ingredients of which has already been used by the Store bomber.
5) The layout of the Store seems greatly to interest the family, judging by the large number of photographic enlargements discovered in a schoolbag belonging to Clara Malaussène, the youngest of the sisters and deliciously minor, during a search of the family's residence, a permit having been obtained on . . . etc.
6) The minorest of all the Malaussène children has been dreaming about "Xmas Ogres" for the last few months, a sinister obsession seemingly connected to the (no less sinister) photographs found on the scene of the latest explosion.
7) The pregnancy of Louna Malaussène, a nurse, the eldest sister and barely major, lies behind the meeting between Benjamin Malaussène and Professor Leonard, the victim of the third explosion.
8) Even the family dog (age and breed unknown) seems linked to the business, since he suffered from a nervous fit on the scene of one of the murders. (An examination of the photos discovered in the Swedish display lavatories has shown that at least one of them features a dog in the throes of a similar attack.)

The light grew brighter once more. Sitting there in front of me, Chief Superintendent Coudrier looked like the only person who was still sparking in Paris's surrounding gloom.

"Rather intriguing, don't you think, for a worn-out squad of police officers dying to make an arrest?"

Silence.

"But that isn't all, Monsieur Malaussène. Would you care to take a look at this?"

He handed me a thick brown envelope, full to bursting point, bearing the insignia of a leading Parisian publishing house.

"We received this yesterday. I was waiting to speak to you about it."

The envelope contained some two to three hundred typewritten pages. They claimed to be a novel, entitled *IMPLOSION* and authored by Benjamin Malaussène. A single glance at it was enough for me to recognise that it was the tale I'd started to spin the kids when this business had begun, and which had been concluded a fortnight previously after Jeremy's confession. I looked so flabbergasted that Coudrier felt it necessary to add:

"We found the original in your flat."

Sleeping Paris snored on around us.

The wailing of a police car broke through it like a bad dream. On Chief Superintendent Coudrier's desk, the light dimmed again slightly.

"Listen to me carefully, my lad . . ."

("My lad", forsooth . . . !)

"The only thing that you still have going for you is my own personal conviction. Meaning, of course, that I am convinced of your innocence. Not one of my men agrees with me. Having them explore other avenues in such conditions is no easy matter. If nothing occurs in the near future to confirm my conviction . . ."

I could hear those dot, dot, dots tumbling down one after the other! That's when I cracked. Too bad for Theo. Too bad for our in-house Zorro. I declared that I'd seen a little old man in a grey smock nick two cartridges from the armaments counter and then use their powder to fill the metal casing of a drill head.

"Why didn't you tell us all this before?"

(Good question.)

"You might have saved a man's life, Monsieur Malaussène."

(Well, you see, it's all because of my mate Theo, Chief Superintendent, my mate Theo and his leek vinaigrette.)

"Nevertheless, we shall still check out the matter."

He didn't seem to have put very much conviction into that. Indeed not, because he then felt he had to add:

"Burn a few candles if you want us to find him . . ."

Chapter 33

"ARE YOU COMPLETELY crazy? Don't you realize what you've done?"

"I wanted it to be a surprise, Ben."

"Well, you've certainly succeeded!"

It's hard to describe how furious I was. Why did it have to be Clara, my Clara, who'd had the idea of photocopying that manuscript and of sending it off to eleven publishers? ELEVEN! (11!)

"You shouldn't work yourself up into a state like that. It's very good, you know. The policemen had a great time reading it."

Wring Louna's neck? Strangle her for butting in in her dreamy voice, with her hands folded over the hemisphere of her soon-to-be motherhood? For a second, I wondered whether not to.

"Especially the portrait you made of Napoleon-Coudrier. They all had a good laugh about that."

"Louna, just shut up please. Let Clara explain herself."

(I couldn't help wondering what the hell these kids had got between their ears? And what about the teenagers? Anyone at home? Was it just mum's offspring that was made that way, or were they all the same? Would someone, anyone, even a teacher, please tell me, please explain it all to me!) The case hadn't even been wound up yet, the coppers had had their eyes on me for months, Jeremy had burnt his school down and lo and behold Clara sends my yarn off to eleven publishers (eleven of them! Clara!), my yarn, the ending of which provided the recipe for that bomb *à la* Jeremy and the secret of how it was made inside the building! WHY?

"It was to make you feel better, Ben."

(Feel better . . .)

"I asked Julia's opinion, and she agreed with me."

(Oh well, what difference did it make having one more nutter around the place?)

"And it's really funny, Ben. Honestly it is. The policemen were all in stitches."

(I'd noticed that. Especially Coudrier . . .)

"So, Louna, why do you think the publishers turned it down, then?" Because that morning, on the breakfast tray which Clara'd brought me, I'd received my first answer. A polite, but firm rejection. The sender admitted that my masterpiece was "extraordinarily imaginative" but regretted that its structure was "somewhat loose" (you're telling me!), wondered if "publishing such a work would be appropriate while a similar affair was still hitting the headlines" (I wondered about that, too) before concluding that "this sort of novel (had) no place in our list".

(Just as well . . .)

"That doesn't mean anything, Ben. There are still ten other publishers left! You know perfectly well that your biggest failing is that you never believe in what you do."

The wild cat inside me froze. It fixed its eyes on Louna's belly. It thought: "In about a fortnight's time I'll have these two to fend for as well." My lips drew back. My fangs glinted dangerously. That was the moment that Thérèse chose to come out with an extraordinarily penetrating psychological theory:

"Aren't you just upset because it was rejected?"

(Doesn't early retirement for big brothers exist?)

That was how things stood with the family. Things weren't looking all that fucking great, as Jeremy would put it, at work either. There wasn't a trace of our cricketty oldster. And not a trace of the boys in blue. I was out on my own. In a minefield. Everything made me jump out of my skin, a door slamming, a heavyish article falling off a counter, anyone shouting louder than usual. Even Miss Hamilton's voice. I was constantly on the verge of collapse. From acute paranoia.

In the Customer Complaints Office, our clientele's grievances brought *real* tears to my eyes and Lehmann, who had to spend ages comforting me, was putting it around that I'd hit the bottle.

"Is it true?" Theo asked. "Wouldn't you rather have a good snort? It's just as bad for your health, but it does make you feel better in the meantime."

And Sainclair was supportive:

"Your job is a depressing one, Monsieur Malaussène. And, to be quite frank, it's a miracle you've kept it up as long as you have. We shall soon find you a different position. As a matter of fact, would being the ground-floor store detective appeal to you? We're thinking of dispensing with Monsieur Cazeneuve's services."

Why had old Jiminy Cricket vanished? Because I'd spotted him? But he'd been going out of his way to be spotted! If Jeremy hadn't had his accident, I could have witnessed every step of his bomb-making. Why then? Because he sensed that Coudrier's two coppers were tailing me? And why had they both vanished on me as well? Why hadn't they been replaced by two others, who faded into the woodwork? There wasn't a single copper left in the Store. Neither Theo, nor his little oldsters had been questioned. Why was I out on a limb like this? What were they trying to do? I needed a bomb. I needed a bomb to go off. I needed to know where, when and who! I badly needed to lay my hands on the fucker who'd been framing me up for the past few months. I needed that. Otherwise, I was going to do time for him. No proof, just a pile of clues and circumstantial evidence. Enough to have me doing porridge until Louna's twins had got the vote. And who was going to bring the little buggers up? Jeremy? He'd just teach them how to make a neutron bomb! Mum? Mum . . .

"Mum, mum . . ."

It was in the showers next to our changing rooms that Theo found me sobbing like a baby: "Mum, mum . . .", hiccuping over the washbasin, dowsing my face with cold water and grizzling my eyes out: "Mum, mum . . .", my despair doubled up by a litany: "Father, why hast thou forsaken me?" which rose up unbidden from the distant days of catechism, when mum had tried to give me a God to make up for not having a dad. "Mum, mum, why hast thou forsaken me?" And Theo comforting me, just like old Amar's Yasmina used to do, Theo, who I'd betrayed by grassing up his little old executioner . . .

"One of my oldsters, you say?"

"One of your oldsters, Theo. The one that looks like a cricket, the one who was messing around with those taps the day the photo booth went off, that's why he was trying to get you away from there, so you wouldn't be hurt in the explosion . . . I grassed him up to the police, Theo, they were getting onto my case too much . . ."

Theo's hand turned the tap off and, since we were in full catechism, he wiped my face with a biblical sweep of a towel. I almost expected my image to appear printed on the other side of it . . .

"It doesn't matter, Ben. Anyway, what with those photos they found in the Swedish bogs, the police are already on the right track."

"What's that old lad's name?"

"No idea. I don't call them by name, I call them by nickname."

"Where's his kip?"

"Christ knows . . . some home or other, or a bedsit somewhere."

"Why has he vanished?"

"Why do people of that age generally vanish, Ben?"

"Do you think he's dead?"

"That happens, yes. What's more, with their unchanging wrinkles, that always comes as a surprise."

"Theo, *don't let him be dead.*"

("Burn a few candles if you want us to find him . . .")

"There is another possibility."

"There is?"

"Maybe he's carried out his contract, Ben. Maybe he's done away with all the ogres, then crept back into the woodwork."

Chapter 34

FOR OVER A week, Julia, Theo and I delved into Paris's OAP underworld, Theo guided by his own gang of oldsters, Julia by her investigative reporter's nose, and me by one or the other, too scared stiff to take the slightest initiative and too panicked to distance myself from their investigations. We tried everywhere and anywhere, from the Sally Army's most rundown dives, to the most upmarket bridge clubs, taking in a good number of shamelessly profit-making organizations: crammed doss-houses, hole-in-the-floor lavatories, transparent soup, opaque management, stagnant running water. Each day, Theo got closer to topping himself and Julia to writing her next article.

"I've discovered something, Ben!"

(Hope quivered in my ancient breast.)

"What, Julia, what?"

"The drug-dealing market of the century. All those little oldsters are getting hustled by pushers!"

(I couldn't care less, Julia, I don't give a fuck, just find *my* little oldster *for me*, forget your job for a while, can't you?)

"They're smacking themselves up like there's no tomorrow, Ben. Which is understandable. They do have a lot to forget – even the future. And when they don't want to forget, that means they want to remember. So double the dose!"

She was now ablaze and I knew from experience that nothing on earth could put out those flames.

"I'm not the only one who's caught on. I've witnessed certain transactions . . . Believe you me, that's where the real drug market now is!"

(Was it really necessary to add another item to my list of worries?)

"Watch yourself, Julia. Be careful."

Not a bit of it. She was now flying. "It's obvious, what with all those quacks who never give them enough medication to ease their pain . . ."

(Julia, for crying out loud, look after me first, will you? ME FIRST, JULIA!)

"And all that with the blessing of the powers that be. After all, an oldster who croaks of an overdose is just a ruin toppling over."

Little by little, Theo started recruiting for the Store, Julia started digging up her next article and I found myself stranded with my problem. High and dry, with Theo's words ringing in my mind: "Maybe he's carried out his contract, Ben, then crept back into the woodwork."

No, Jiminy Cricket hadn't carried out his contract. He still had one ogre left to exterminate. The sixth and final one. He told me so himself. Yesterday evening. When he came and sat down opposite me on the leatherette seat of a late-night métro, as cool as a cucumber, even though I'd given up all hope of ever finding him. My little cricket-like oldster.

Let's skip my astonishment and get straight into the dialogue:

"The last one?"

"Yes, young fellow my lad. There were six of them. Six people who called themselves 'The Chapel of 111'."

"Why 111?"

"Because 111 multiplied by six equals 666, which is the Number of the Beast, and 111 was the number of victims they were to sacrifice."

He smiled indulgently.

"Yes, symbolic numbers, young fellow. All nonsense. The worst horror always leads to such childish games."

Fine. So, let's get back to the surprise. Jiminy Cricket quite simply sat himself down in front of me. He put his index finger to his lips so that my surprised yell would not escape.

He smiled.

He said:

"Yes, it's really me."

Apart from us, there were three people in the carriage, each one asleep. I'd just parted from Stojil, who hadn't been able to do much for my mood. All he'd done was to repeat to me again and again:

"He can't be that far off, lad, believe me. All real killers start haunting themselves."

"What is a 'real killer', Stojil?"

"Someone who kills on a full stomach."

And so, lo and behold, I had my killer with his full stomach sitting there in front of me.

He perched himself on the seat like a dwarf clambering up onto a throne, wriggling his buttocks to get into the right position. His legs dangled in mid-air, like the kids' legs hanging from their bunks. And his eyes shone as brilliantly as theirs. He no longer had his orphan's grey smock on, but an old man's Terylene coat, falling down in severe folds. The purple badge of the Légion d'Honneur glistened in his buttonhole. Dispensing with any introduction, he started straight into his explanations. Not for a moment did he imagine that I might jump him, strap him up and hand him over bound and gagged to Coudrier. The thought never even occurred to me. As he spoke, he grew larger and, as I listened, I shrank. In the end, his story wasn't that surprising. He told it without striving for effect, going straight to the heart of the matter. (And it was a heart that stank of carrion!) 1942: closure of the Store for a European pogrom. All the same, the legal ins and outs did still take six months. The owners went out of their way to defend themselves, and civilization played at playing it by the book. But these six months led, of course, to the gaping maw of the gas chambers. "History settled their score", as that shit-head Risson put it, from behind the great wall of his books. Exit the management.

1942: six months during which our department store was abandoned to the silent half-light of its plenty. Goods hibernating through the war and, all around them, the Militia's black *cordon sanitaire*. Certain brown-shirted theorists even claimed that the Store should be kept closed like a tomb until the Millennium of National Socialism.

"They spoke about it as if it were tomorrow, young fellow, convinced that by gobbling up Europe they had annexed Time itself."

And, it happened that within a few weeks, the Store became wrapped up in a pyramid of mysteries. Its unlit immobility attracted rumours like a corpse attracts flies. People whispered the most extraordinary stories about the secret goings-on within it. Some said it was a headquarters of the Resistance, others that it was an experimental theatre for Gestapo torture techniques, others still that it remained what it always had been, but had now suddenly become a stranger, a closed museum to a dead era. Whichever way, people looked at it as if they didn't recognise it any more.

"Nothing becomes legendary more quickly than a public place that the public can no longer frequent!"

So, during that period, imaginations ran rife over the infinite field of legendary possibilities. Within a few months, a millennium had actually passed by in everyone's memory. It was at that time of vibrant eternity that the six ogres of "The Chapel of 111" lived, in the secrecy of that dimly lit world crammed with fossilized merchandise.

"Who were they?"

"You know as well as I do. Six individuals from different backgrounds, brought together by their mutual scorn for what Aleister Crowley called 'the Twentieth Century's sordid abortions', but firmly resolved to take the greatest possible advantage of the pandemonium that had been let loose."

"Professor Leonard was one of them?"

"He was. He was the one who particularly claimed to be an adept of Aleister Crowley. While another said that he followed Gilles de Rays, and so on, but they had all been united into a demonic syncretism which they saw as being the spirit of the age. That's right, young fellow. They were the *spirit of their age*, a spirit which fed on living flesh."

"Of children?"

"And of animals, too, sometimes. Including a dog, which Leonard tore to pieces with his bare teeth."

(So, my poor old Julius, that's what your soul sniffed out! If I told anybody, they'd never believe me . . .)

"How did they come by their victims?"

"During famines, Gilles de Rays used to unlock his larders to attract children. Our six used to lure them into the Kingdom of Toys."

(Xmas Ogres . . .)

"Most of the children had been entrusted by parents at risk to an organization which was to give them safe passage to Spain, and thence to the USA, far away from the massacre then in progress. In fact, the safe passage finished up in the darkness of the Store. And it is the sixth man, the last, the procurer of children, who must now die."

"When?"

The question popped out, just like that, though I was immediately certain that nothing in the world would make him answer it.

"On the 24th of this month."

He smiled across at me. And calmly repeated himself:

"On the 24th, at five thirty p.m., in the toy department. You'll be there, young fellow. As will Chief Superintendent Coudrier, I imagine."

My Jiminy made us change métros six times. His footfalls were echoless in the tiled corridors. It was then that I noticed his slippers. "Old age . . ." he murmured with an apologetic smile.

He answered all my questions. Including the million-dollar one, the one that contained all the others:

"Why have you involved me in this vengeance?"

The métro was bouncing us around the Goutte d'Or. Blacks were nodding in the night. Sleepy heads on watchful shoulders.

"Why me?"

He took a long look at me, as though he was consulting some interior register, then finally replied:

"Because you are a saint."

As I stared dumbly back at him, he developed his thesis:

"You do a wonderful job at the Store, a *totally human* job."

(I do, do I?)

"By assuming everyone else's mistakes, by bearing all the sins of commerce on your shoulders, you are behaving like a saint, even like Christ! . . ."

(Christ? Me? Jesus!)

"I had been waiting so long for you . . ."

All the Whitsun tongues of fire suddenly lit up in his eyes. And so it was, all ablaze from the inside, that he explained to me why he made bombs go off under my nose. According to him, absolute evil had to be destroyed before the eyes of its diametric opposite, true goodness, the Scapegoat, the symbol of persecuted innocence: yours truly. That's right, the Saint *had to witness* the destruction of those demons.

"And you will witness it, young fellow. You are the sole depository of the truth, the only person worthy of it!"

I hardly need to say that, no sooner had I abandoned my cricket to the Paris night than I dived into a phone box and called up Coudrier. He listened to me without a word of interruption, then said:

"I did tell you that you had a dangerous job . . ."

(Not for much longer, saints preserve us!)

"The 24th, at five thirty p.m. in the toy department, you say? That's Thursday. I'll be there and you try to be there, too, Monsieur Malaussène."

"No way!"

"In that case, nothing will happen and you will still be my squad's number one suspect."

OK. But still I asked him:

"Do you have any idea who this procurer of children, the last victim, might be?"

"Not the slightest. How about you?"

"All he said was that I'd be surprised."

"Very well. Then let us wait for the surprise."

Julius was waiting for me at the foot of my bed. Julius, who'd sniffed out far more than I had in all this business. Julius, who'd answered all the questions. Julius, who still hadn't been given his bath. I stroked his head, as it ticked over, and let my own drop from a great height onto the pillow. Where it received an icy slap from the glossy cover of a magazine.

It was the issue of *Actuel*.

The one that told the life of the Saint. Out at last!

I opened it on the pages which concerned me and, to be perfectly honest, had rather mixed feelings about it. If ever my old Zorro with his Légion d'Honneur read all that, then he'd have quite another think about my saintly status.

On the other hand, the thought of the expression on Sainclair's gob made me extremely happy. And absolutely delighted at the idea of being fired, rid at last of that filthy job. Because police inquiries or no police inquiries, Sainclair was definitely going to have to give me the boot now!

For the first time in ages (and despite the prospect of Thursday coming) I fell to sleep like one of the just.

Chapter 35

"DO YOU HAVE any children, Malaussène?"

His face was a mask. He received me in his office, just like the last time. Only he didn't offer me a whisky or a cigar. Or even a seat. And this time there were no congratulations. He just asked:

"Do you have any children?"

"I don't know."

"Then you had better find out. Because I'm going to sue you and you're going to lose and be ruined unto the seventh generation. You owe it to any possible heirs to inform them of this fact."

The issue of *Actuel* was lying there, open in front of him. But he was looking at me.

"Trying to piss on our fireworks is a common enough thing to do and it would certainly have cost you a pretty penny. But now you've emptied your entire bladder . . ."

He did a bit of rapid mental arithmetic . . .

"It's going to cost you the earth, Monsieur Malaussène."

The smile which I wanted to wipe off his face sprang back onto it with elastic efficiency. The sort of efficiency which two-bit saints like me could do with.

"Because what you seem to forget is that you signed a contract. And this contract clearly describes your job as that of a quality controller. So, when the time comes, you will find yourself up against 855 employees who will all swear – before almighty God – that you never did your job properly, that you preferred grovelling like a martyr, a role you dreamt up in your own sick imagination, and that if the

Store did anything wrong, then it was to keep you on our books for such a long time."

A pause.

"In the three years since I took over the management of the Store, not a single employee has been dismissed."

With a blossoming flush of that smile, he repeated:

"Not a single one."

(He really did seem to have only one sort of smile.)

"Which is why we kept you on."

His voice now contained another ingredient. Something which gives the Sainclairs of this world their strength: *he believed what he was saying.* He firmly believed in the version of things that he'd just concocted. It wasn't *his* truth, it was *the* truth. The one that keeps the tills merrily ticking over. The only one.

"There's something else."

(Yes, Sainclair?)

"If I were you, I'd watch your back. Because if I were one of the customers who had dealings with you during the last six months, then I rather think I would try to find you . . . No matter how long that might take."

(I then saw a back rise up in front of me. A back fit to eclipse the sun: "Don't let those shit-heads get you, my lad, get them first!")

"That will be all."

(How do you mean, "all"?)

"You can go now. You're fired."

That was where I tripped up, by murmuring in a wily tone:

"But you told me that the police had forbidden any hiring or firing during their inquiries . . ."

He gave a beautiful managerial laugh.

"Are you joking? I quite simply lied to you, Malaussène, in the interests of the Store, that is. You were doing an excellent job at the time and I didn't want you to resign."

(Jolly good. Jolly jolly good . . . Screwed, in other words. He'd screwed me.)

And, while he was kindly showing me out:

"As a matter of fact, we're not entirely losing you. You used to save us a lot of money, and now you are going to earn us even more."

That's the way it goes. You're expecting to get off on the hit of the century, and when it comes it's as bitter as sucked lemons. Julia had been right about that, as she had been about certain other things: never invest in future pleasures. It's now or never. Just go and see our Rusky neighbours and ask them about their radiant future . . .

Thus was I philosophizing to myself as I walked in front of Lehmann's eyes for the last time. Ah! that look of betrayal which he gave me from his transparent cage, as the escalator plunged me down into the depths . . . Shame! Shame on you! But I should have been over the moon!

I was so out of it, that I nearly fell flat on my face when the moving staircase reached the unmoving floor. And, when I got my balance back (through the giggles of the little toy salesgirls) it was to hear Miss Hamilton's ethereal voice sparkling with a brand new smile:

"Monsieur Cazeneuve is requested at the Customer Complaints Office."

In everyone's daily round, there should be a special time set aside for feeling sorry for yourself. A specific time, which is not taken up by working, by feeding your face, or by digestion, a moment of total freedom, a gap during which you can clearly measure the true extent of the catastrophe. Once that was out of the way, the day would then be better, illusions swept away, the landscape plainly marked out. But if you think over your misfortunes between two mouthfuls of your lunch, with the horizon clouded over by the work which is shortly to be done, you get your wires crossed and your sums wrong, you think you're even worse off than you really are. Sometimes you even think you're happy!

That was what I'd been daydreaming about, laid flat out on my bed, with Julius lending me his body heat, just two seconds ago, before the phone rang. I felt just fine. I was inching my way over the full extent of my balls-up, savouring that taste of defeat which my victory over Sainclair had been turned into. I was about to get the exact dimensions of my secret garden of disgust fixed in my mind, when that frigging bell suddenly messed up all my calculations and had me make that gesture which is, more than any other, nourished on illusions: I picked up the receiver.

"Ben? Louna has now arrived at term."

"Arrived at term" . . . Only Thérèse could come out with something like that. When I kick the bucket, instead of being devastated at my death, she'll say that she's "been deeply affected by the sad demise of her elder brother".

Right then. So Louna had "arrived at term". I copied down the maternity's clinical white address, let myself slide into the métro, grabbed hold of the handrail and waited for it all to be over. The idea of discovering those brand new twins' faces (or face?) was beating inside me. Before long, it was beating just as hard as it had done five years back when Half Pint came along, and even further back with Jeremy, and further still with Clara – I was her reception committee (the midwife was pissed and the quack had taken the money and run), I was the one who cut my Clara's little mooring rope and who showed her round her new home, with mum off in the background, already repeating: "You're a good son, Benjamin, you've always been a good son . . ."

That's right. What I felt was happiness. Well, sort of. All the dimensions I'd measured when laid out on my bed were now well and truly out of focus. But I still did my best to think straight. "Louna's arrived at term", what a lovely euphemism to cover what was, in fact, the beginning of a new series of disasters. Because there was no getting away from it, those twins meant two more mouths to feed, four more ears to entertain, twenty more fingers to keep tabs on, and one hell of a lot of tears to mop up, again and again and again! And, on top of all that, there was Sainclair's court case in the offing, bankruptcy looming, perhaps even prison, dishonour for sure and (here I come, Zola!) the slippery slope of alcoholism. Sod it! What I'd do would be to put the twins out on the street, as soon as they'd reached the age of five. That's what I'd do! Amputations and begging bowls! And they'd better rake it in, if they wanted anything more to chew on than their empty plates!

Why did "reality" get in the way of all my schemes? Why did life have it in for me? That's what I was wondering as I stood beside Louna's bed, in that clinic full of screams and flowers, gazing at Laurent who was hugging my sister: "My darling, my love, my darling, my love," then pressing his nose up against that disinfected aquarium, specially designed to protect babies against starving fathers, and bawling:

"I've got three Lounas, three Lounas, Ben! I used to have one, and now I've got three!"

(But not for the price of one, believe you me!)

We ended up in the Koutoubia with Amar giving us a couscous on the house, as he always does when I arrive bearing news of a birth.

"I've made an important discovery, Ben." (This was Laurent getting philosophical over a 16° glass of Mascara.) "Which is that what happens is always easier to bear than what may happen in the future, even if it turns out to be worse! I didn't want a kid, now I've got two, but that isn't the worst of it, Ben, no, the worst thing is that I was afraid of such a wonderful event." (Sighs.) "Oh, Ben! How could I have done that to Louna?" (Sobs.) "Smash my face in, Ben, I beg of you, smash my face in, do it for your sister!" (Self-flagellation, rending of shirt . . .)

"Another drop of Mascara?"

"Yes please, it isn't a bad year, you know."

"Ben?"

Julia's hand encircled my thigh.

"Clara told me about the court case, and you shouldn't worry. Sainclair was having you on. If he does take legal action, then it will be against the magazine, and if the judge is a particularly unpleasant one, then he'll make us pay one franc's token damages."

"A pre-revaluation franc at that. A micro franc. A centime," Theo added, ogling Hadouch's buttocks.

The evening purred away, with Clara cutting up Jeremy's meat for him, Thérèse leaning over the jukebox playing Umm Kulthum's funeral again and again, Half Pint introducing Julius to the ritual of mint tea and Amar telling us for the umpteenth time that his restaurant was about to be swamped over by the construction of the New Belleville.

"I'm sorry about that, Amar."

"Why? Rest is a good thing, my son."

And on he went telling me how he'd make the most of his retirement and nurse his rheumatism by bathing in the sands of the southern Sahara. (Amar's white head, with the Sahara wrapped round his neck . . .)

And it was at the very end of the proceedings (with a dead-drunk Laurent snoozing in his plate, Jeremy and Half Pint rolled up in a ball nestling under Julius's fur, Theo long gone with Hadouch, Thérèse transformed into a whirling dervish, and Julia's hand about to unleash the final assault) when Clara, my Clara, told me the big news.

"I've got a surprise for you, Benjamin."

Chapter 36

THE SURPRISE (did I really still like surprises?) came in the shape of a telegram. And the telegram from a famous publishing house (if I don't name names, it's to make them all tear each other's eyes out . . .). It was couched in the following terms, so concise as almost to be a sub-poena:

"EXTREMELY INTERESTED, COME AT ONCE."

Discovering that you're a genius despite yourself is rather pleasant. It was quite a buzz to think that a few months of inconsequential blathering, cooked up for a bunch of sleepless kids and an epileptic dog, typed out by a relentlessly accurate secretary, then dispatched by an irresponsible messenger girl, were enough to get this publishing dragon's mouth watering.

That's what I said to myself when I woke up. That's what I told myself when down in the métro. That's what I was still telling myself while dragging my heels in this immense (office? salon? lecture hall? race track?), in which ancient history's gilded panelling flirted with the daring geometry of avant-garde furniture. Aluminium and stucco, go-getterism and tradition, offices stuffed full of the past and all set to stuff down the future. I could have ended up in a worse tip.

The punctilious politeness of the snappy dresser who showed me in confirmed my impression that they were waiting for me, and for me alone. Since they'd sent the telegram, no-one had slept a wink. Something in the air told me that the entire place was holding its breath.

"What if Malaussène says no?"

A wind of panic across the meeting-room table.

"What if he's received other offers?"

"In that case, gentlemen, we'll quintuple their price . . ."

(*Implosion* . . . Clara's title wasn't that bad after all.)

"Can I offer you something to drink?"

The smoothy had made a minibar spring out from the depths of a bookcase.

"Scotch? Port?"

(Just the moment for a drop of port, no? Sure it was.)

"A cup of coffee."

No problem. A cup of coffee. A pregnant pause. A crossing of legs. A long stare from the smoothy. My little spoon described a silver circle.

"Truly extra-ordinary, Monsieur Malaussène."

(Extraordinary is normally written as one word.)

"But I am not allowed to tell you any more."

A simper.

"That's a pleasure which our Literary Director is reserving for herself."

Simper.

"An extra-ordinary person, as you will see . . ."

(Her too?)

"Between you and me, everyone here calls her Queen Zabo."

(OK for Queen Zabo, just between you and me.)

"An unerring judgment, and a frank way with words . . ."

A moment's hesitation, then, half a tone lower:

"And that's just where the problem lies."

(Problem? What problem?)

A smile, a clearing of his throat, the outward signs of upper-crust embarrassment, then, all of a sudden:

"Very well. Then I shall tell her that you're here."

Exit the smoothy. Then half an hour went by. Half an hour of waiting for Queen Zabo's arrival. To start with, I told myself that the books would keep me amused. I meekly stood in front of the bookcase, respectfully put out my hand and gingerly removed a volume: an empty jacket. No book inside.

I tried elsewhere. Same story.

There wasn't a single book in the place! Nothing but those shelves of brightly painted dust-jackets. There was no doubt about it, Malaussène, you were definitely at a publisher's.

I contented myself by totting up how much my best-seller would make. If you added everything in: the film rights, the TV serial, readings on the radio, then it was incalculable. If you only went for the bare minimum, then it still short-circuited my mental arithmetic. Whatever the result, how right I had been to get rid of that stinking goat's job. Thirty years of my salary wouldn't even be worth a tenth of my royalties!

Queen Zabo chose just that precise moment of bliss to make her entrance. Queen Zabo!

"Ah, good morning, Monsieur Malaussène!"

She was a tall scrawny woman, with an obese head planted on top.

(Good morning, madam . . .)

"No, don't get up. In any case, I shan't be keeping you long . . ."

A shrill voice which didn't go in for please and thank you.

"So?"

This "so" was screamed out, making me jump. (So what, your Highness?) I must have been looking pretty flabbergasted, because she burst out into a jowl-wobbling laugh. How weird! It really did look as if that head had landed on her shoulders quite by chance!

"Oh no, Monsieur Malaussène, let there be no misunderstanding between us. I didn't ask you to come here because of your book. We don't publish that sort of bland bullshit!"

The smoothy, who was acting the Page, cleared his throat. Queen Zabo span round through 180 degrees.

"Bland bullshit. That was your opinion, wasn't it, Gauthier?"

Then, turning back to me:

"Look, Monsieur Malaussène, it isn't a book that you've got there.

There's no aesthetic sense to it. It wanders around from one thing to another, then ends up nowhere at all. And you'll never do any better than that. Give it up at once, my old chap, that is not where your talents lie!"

Gauthier the Page would dearly have liked to vanish through a hole in the floor. As for me, Queen Zabo was starting to have an effect on my innards.

"Here's where they really lie!"

She threw the current issue of *Actuel* down onto my lap. Where the hell had that sprung from? Her hands had been empty when she came in, hadn't they?

"You just cannot imagine how much a publisher could do with someone like you. A Scapegoat! It's exactly what I need. Really, Monsieur Malaussène, I'm sick and tired of fielding all the brickbats myself!"

There then followed a long, high-pitched wave of laughter, which sounded like an unstoppable leak of something unpleasant. Then it suddenly stopped.

"Between the apprentice writers who think they are being misunderstood, the novice writers who think they are being misrepresented and the experienced writers who think they are being misused, everyone yells at me, Monsieur Malaussène! Not once, do you hear me? not once in twenty years of publishing have I ever met a writer who was satisfied with his lot!"

Our Queen Zabo put me in mind of a child prodigy, aged fifty, who still can't believe how bright she is. But there was something else about her. Something irredeemably sad lurking behind all that forced gaiety. Yes, something lying beneath the electrical mass of her flabby face.

"For example, Monsieur Malaussène, just last week a candidate came round to see what we thought of the manuscript which he'd sent us two months before. It was nine in the morning. Gauthier, here present (you are still present, aren't you, Gauthier?), asked him into his office and bumbled off in a doze to fetch the reader's report from my files; in fact it was in his own all the time. During his absence, our friend quite naturally started rummaging through his papers. He came across the report, on which I'd written 'A heap of shit'. That's right. Amongst ourselves we are all terribly to the point. Gauthier's job, in fact, consists in wrapping up this succinctness. Anyway, that report was not supposed to have been seen by the author of the manuscript in question. So, Monsieur Malaussène, what do you suppose his reaction was?"

(Eh, well, dunno really . . .)

"He went and chucked himself in the Seine, right opposite us, over there."

With a lightning gesture, she indicated the bay window overlooking the river.

"And he still had that report, with my name to it, in his hand when they fished him out. All highly unpleasant."

Then, all at once, I twigged what was wrong about her. Once upon a time, Queen Zabo had been a sensitive soul, a little girl who suffered for the ills of the entire world. A tormented adolescent. Something along those lines. The mysterious martyr to *life's sorrows*. When her torments had become too much for her, she went along, after a deal of hesitation, to lie down on a fashionable shrink's couch. The Great Listener had sussed out at once that what was cramping that livewire's style was her humanity. So, session after session, he patiently plucked it out by the roots and planted social adaptability in its place. That was Queen Zabo for you: a successful shrink-case. When she eats, it's only her head that gets nourishment. The rest is disconnected. I'd met others like her. They were all pretty much the same.

"So, Monsieur Malaussène, I intend to take you on so as to avoid any further unpleasantness of that sort."

(Me? I wasn't being taken on! No way!) Silence. An x-ray stare from Her Highness, then:

"I imagine that the Store fired you after an article such as this one. Aren't I right?"

An ultra-violet gaze. The suggestion of a smile:

"Perhaps that was even why you had it published?"

Then, firmly:

"You're being ridiculous, Monsieur Malaussène. You're the man for the job, and for no other job. Being a Scapegoat is a basic part of your *nature.*"

Then, while escorting me outside at a rate of knots:

"Don't fool yourself, now. You're obviously going to receive a pile of job offers. However much they want to pay you, just remember, we'll double it."

Chapter 37

AND THEN THAT fatal Thursday arrived. I did my best to slow down the flow of time by concentrating on each second. Nothing doing. It still ended up seeping through the cracks in my saintly soul.

The toy department was certainly far from being crowded out. An order must have been handed down; a sign which mysteriously kept the customers away. I was there. And I realized that I hadn't stopped thinking about this moment for a single second since my little underground excursion the other night with Jiminy Cricket. This deadline had been an obsession, carefully concealed inside my every thought. I was frightened. Christ, was I frightened! It was five thirty p.m. Jiminy hadn't turned up yet. Neither had Coudrier. Nor had any of his men.

My little squirrel salesgirl had lost weight. Her cheeks no longer contained her winter provisions. It was the Store . . . the fatigue of the Store . . . Her friend, the weasel, was busy putting the displays back into order, after they'd been wrecked by the four o'clock tidal wave of kids. Jiminy wasn't there.

But I was.

And what about the victim? Was the victim there? "I'll point him out to you at the last minute. You'll see, it's going to be quite a surprise . . ." Why a surprise? Deep down, that was the thing I couldn't stop thinking about. (Why a surprise? Did that mean that I knew the victim? Was it a public figure? A media personality?) I thought about that and I thought about the rest of the business, all heaped together. About our chat in the métro. "Why do you kill them in the Store?

Do you lure them there? How?" My little oldster had smiled sweetly. "Do you ever read novels?" I answered that I did and more than just sometimes. "Then you should know that all the surprises in a story mustn't be divulged at once." I thought how "divulged" sounded like a word belonging to his generation. But I also thought: "story"? "Story"? "Exactly. Just imagine that you're part of a novel. It will help you to cope with your fear." Then he added: "Maybe even to enjoy it." That's when I started to find him a touch odd. And to feel scared. A lurking panic which hadn't left me for a second and which was now having physical effects. Quite literally scaring me shitless. That was real fear for you. I wondered how he'd got onto me. And Thérèse . . . How the fuck had he spotted and identified Thérèse? "Of your brothers and sisters, she's the one who resembles you most." (Ah! So he knew the others as well, did he?) Yes, he did. Half Pint and his Xmas Ogres, Jeremy and his gift for experimental science, Clara's eye . . . "There's nothing mysterious about that, young fellow, your friend Theo adores you all." Of course, Theo! Theo had told him about us. "You are, in a sense, his family. Just as he is ours, too." Ours? Ah, yes, meaning the Store's little old men. All the same, it was that which had made me come there, that day, and not Coudrier's warning on the phone. It was the fact that I sensed a strange menace hovering over my family, if ever I tried to disappear. What's more, I still had a real soft spot for my mythical granddad, the gobbler-up of ogres, no matter how loopy he was.The métro had been shaking us up like life itself and, to keep balance on his bum, he'd leant on the palms of his hands, with his arms stretched out at either side of him. Like the stabilizers on a kid's bike.

That's right, I was well into the idea of making off with my oldster, of setting him up at home as a stand-in forebear, had it not been for this business with the bombs and our god-damn appointment. Because, after all, sitting there on his little behind, he was asking me to come along and witness a murder . . .

"And you will witness it, young fellow. You are the only person worthy of it!"

* * *

There he was. He'd arrived. He'd put on one of the grey smocks belonging to Theo's little oldsters. He was making himself look just as senile as the rest of them. He had become that tiny slobbering old man again. The one with the AMX 30. It was impossible to work out if he'd seen me or not. There he was at the other end of the department. He was messing around with that robotic King Kong which, what with the swooning woman in its arms, had managed to get me feeling so down after I'd diddled the deep-sea diver. So I upped my periscope and looked for any sign of coppers in the Store. Sod all. There was a scattering of customers, hunting down merchandise, unaware of the drama now being played out. And what about the victim? No victim to be seen either. At least, nobody I recognised. Fuck you, Coudrier, you two-bit Napoleon, don't do a Grouchy on me! Show up, will you! I was half dead with shitlessness. I didn't want to witness a murder. I didn't want the killers to get killed. I'd never wanted that! I was dead against it! For Christ's sake, Coudrier, get your arse in gear! Do your police bit! Nick old Zorro and his prey! Decorate the former and chuck the latter out with the trash, just leave me out of it! I was the honest brother of a large family and not the long arm of the law! Nor its peepers, either! COUDRIER! WHERE ARE YOU?

(If anyone had ever told me that, one day, I'd be that keen for the boys in blue to show up! . . .)

Jiminy spotted me.

He smiled.

Behind his dribbling old fool act, he gestured at me to wait and not be impatient. He went on playing like a kid with that black ape which was holding an unconscious Clara's snow-white body in its arms. He put it down at his feet and set it off in my direction. The evil ape got moving. That's right. Let's play. Just the right moment for it! A little patience . . .

(I decided to split. No way I was going to hang around there. Split! If, in five seconds, I didn't see the Emperor with his Old Guard turning up, then I'd scarper!)

One . . .

Two . . .

Three . . .

Then a sudden flash of inspiration. I KNEW WHO THE VICTIM WAS! It was that shit-head Risson! The bookseller of my dreams! It all fitted: his age, his diseased brain, his presence there at the Store forty years back. He was the procurer! The procurer of children! The tempter, who'd hoodwinked endangered families into thinking he was going to spirit their kiddies out of the combat zone, while he was actually replenishing the ogres' larder! He was the only person I knew who fitted the part! Risson. He was going to show up at any moment, mysteriously attracted by the scent of his own death. He was going to blow up before my very eyes! If I legged it, then he'd still get splattered. I was sure of that. To be the saintly mark of approval for this execution, all that I needed to know were the time and the place! On the last occasion, Zorro had been quite content with Thérèse's presence. No, I couldn't leave. I was no killer. I'd have liked to have been one, it no doubt made life easier, but it just didn't fit into my saintly character. I'd stay there. Keep playing with the wandering gorilla for as long as it took. I'd wait. Stay alert. Then, when Risson showed up, I'd jump him and throw him out of this minefield. Let Justice then sort him out, but without me. Since I wasn't the Crime, I wasn't the Judge either!

That flashing gorilla had a penguin's charming waddle. This false innocence added to its sinister nature. Its red eyes. The fire in its mouth. Clara in its arms . . . Stop bullshitting, Malaussène. It wasn't the right moment! When it got to my feet, I turned it round back towards him. I had to make this stupid fucking game last. *Make it last!* That meant everything. Until something happened. Until Coudrier appeared, or until Risson's tall, distinguished figure came rolling over the horizon of the escalator. Wasn't that ape's fur black! And wasn't that girl's body white! The flash of white flesh against the darkness of night! The flames in its mouth and the sinister gleam in its eyes . . .

Then suddenly I saw his eyes over there, Jiminy's, staring at me. Smiling at me. My mythical granddad . . .

And I understood.

It had taken me long enough!

A lifetime.

At least.

It was the same stare as Leonard's! The same eyes as the Beast's!

And he was sending me my own death.

The surprise and the fear were so intense that the sword of fire went straight through my head again. A whole kebab skewer of bleeding oysters was wrenched out of my skull.

Deaf again. And then, of course, I spotted Coudrier. Ten yards away. Just beside a tailor's dummy dressed like him, as motionless and as rigid. Coudrier. Caregga in among the leather jackets. And a few others. A sudden police presence.

The gorilla had advanced another yard or so.

Why me?

And weren't those evil dwarf's eyes over there gleaming with delight!

He'd understood that I'd understood.

Then suddenly I did understand.

He was the sixth one, the last one, the procurer! For some reason that was beyond me, he'd wiped out all the others.

And now he was going to blow me away.

Why? His Highness Kong got nearer. Caregga glanced questioningly at Coudrier, whose right hand was stuck under his lapel. Coudrier rapidly shook his head.

No? What did he mean, "no"? Yes, damn you! Yes! Draw, Caregga! There was a bluish tint in the sparks flying off that gorilla. Blue and yellow which brought out its bloody redness.

A lost look at Coudrier.

An unheard, unspoken prayer to Caregga.

Frozen impetus.

No answer.

And that indescribable glee on the old man's face.

That joy sparked off by the sight of my terror. An orgasm! The buzz of a lifetime! If he'd had to draw out his life just to wait for that moment, then it had been worth a hundred years' wait!

Coudrier wasn't going to intervene.

The extra-lucid mutt inside me confirmed that fact to the all-seeing one.

They were all going to let me take a dive!

So if I was going to dive, I'd well and truly dive!

The dive of a lifetime. Straight at that child-snatching ape! I clearly saw my own body, parallel to the floor, as if I was someone else. I dived on that ape, but without taking my eyes off him, over there, the smirking ogre. And when I hit my target . . .

When I pressed the button . . . He was the one who exploded.

Over there.

At the other end of the counter.

His grey smock inflated.

For a second, his face reached the apogee of pleasure.

Then a bloody mess spilled out from his smock. What had been his body.

Implosion.

And when I got to my feet again, I realized he'd turned me into a murderer.

Why me?

Why?

The police took me away.

Chapter 38

THIS TIME, IT took me hours to get my hearing back. Hours spent on my own in what must have been a noisy hospital bedroom. Alone, if you didn't count the thirty-odd medical students who were religiously lapping up every word of their white-coated master as he dwelt on my condition of recurrent bouts of deafness. He smiled a Knowledgeable Smile. They all looked like serious apprentices. One day, they'd end up massacring one another to be able to step into his shoes. He would cling on desperately to his stethoscope. All of this would take place far away from me. Because with six murders on my back, I would then be ticking off the days of six life sentences.

"Why?"

Why me?

Why frame me up?

Jiminy was no longer there to answer.

What was my ideal granddad's name, in fact? I didn't even know what he was called.

If I could only stay deaf through to the bitter end. But our white-coated master hadn't bribed his way through his exams. So he obviously ended up by unblocking me.

"There is no actual lesion, ladies and gentlemen."

Admiring rhubarb from the knowledge-gobbling piranhas.

"And the symptoms will now never reappear again."

Then to me, in his suavely fragrant voice:

"You're cured, my dear chap. I'm pleased to say that you're free to go."

* * *

My freedom immediately led to the appearance of Inspector Caregga. Who, without a word, took me to police headquarters, Quai des Orfèvres. (Why give me back my hearing and then hand me over to a mute?)

Car doors slammed. Staircases. Lift. The clicking of heels down corridors. Office doors banged. Then a knock, knock, knock on Chief Superintendent Coudrier's door.

He was on the phone. He hung up. He stared at me while slowly shaking his head. He asked:

"Coffee?"

(Why not?)

"Elisabeth, if you please . . ."

Coffee.

"Thank you. You can leave us now."

(That's right. Just leave the coffee-pot. There. That's it.)

When it closed behind Elisabeth, Chief Superintendent Coudrier's door was the only one in the entire building that didn't slam.

"So, my lad. Have you finally grasped it all?"

(Not really, no.)

"You're free to go. I've just telephoned your family to reassure them."

Then came the explanations. The final explanations. Thus: I wasn't a murderer. But that fire and brimstone runt who I'd blown to smithereens certainly was. And quite a murderer at that! Not only had he brought about his own death by tricking me into diving onto that gorilla, but he had also wiped out the rest of his team of ogres.

"How did he lure them into the Store?"

I asked that question quite spontaneously and it had, in fact, been what had troubled Coudrier for some time.

"He didn't lure them there. They came of their own free will."

"Sorry?"

"Suicides, Monsieur Malaussène."

He suddenly smiled and stretched himself out in his chair.

"This business has taken thirty years off me. Care for another cup?"

* * *

There had been no end of two-bit sects like that during the slaughterhouse of the Second World War. And, once peace had been signed, one of Chief Superintendent Coudrier's first jobs had been to scrub out those devil's cauldrons.

"A fairly tedious task, my lad. Those awful 1940s sects were as alike as two drops of blood."

They were, in fact, all based on the same model. That strange phenomenon which resulted in the rejection of both moral values and of ideology for the mystical belief in the Moment. *Everything is permitted because everything is possible.* That was more or less what they had between their ears. And the excesses of the period encouraged them. They ended up imitating what was going on around them. In addition, there was a radical critique of materialism, as something which made mankind at once dependent and provident – commerce bringing about an abject faith in tomorrow's profits. Death to tomorrow! Long live the Moment! And glory be to orgasmic Mammon, the Prince of the Eternal Moment! There. That was pretty much what was in the air. And so, here and there, various period loonies got together to form instant sects which were both orgiastic and murderous, including our Chapel of 111, a merry gang of ogres who were adepts of *Beast N° 666.*

"I must admit that I was all at sea to start off with."

But Coudrier had then caught on pretty sharpish.

"The first indication was that orgasmic expression on the faces of all the victims."

That's right, the first one with his gaping flies, or the two old dears snogging away, our pro-lifer giving himself one off the wrist before popping his clogs, and that naked German in the Scandinavian crappers . . .

"There was something not quite *normal* about it all."

(Not quite, no.)

Sex and death rang bells with the Chief Superintendent. *Tod und Sex* stank of arse-about religious antics, an odour he'd learnt to recognise during his post-war investigations.

"But why did they choose the Store for their . . . ceremonies?"

"I've told you why. To their way of thinking, the Store stood for a temple to materialistic desires. So they decided to profane it by sacrificing innocent victims who had been lured there by the attraction of objects. Helmut Künz, the German, used to like dressing up as Father Xmas, as is shown in his collection of photos. He used to hand toys round during the ritual . . ."

Silence. My soul had iced over. (Coffee, please. A small cup of lovely, warm coffee!)

"Why did they commit suicide?"

Good question. His eyes lit up.

"As for their suicides, it was your sister Thérèse and her astrological deductions which put me on the right track. These gentlemen listened to the stars. They firmly believed that the times of their deaths were written there. By killing themselves on the appointed day, they were respecting their astral destinies, while conserving their freedom as individuals."

"They were appropriating the role of Fate, so to speak . . ."

"That's right. By blowing themselves up in public, in the very place where they had lived out their most intense experiences, they gave themselves their last dose of pleasure. A sort of apotheosis."

"Hence the look of ecstasy on their dead faces."

A nod. Silence. (Simple souls, when it came down to it . . .)

"But what about me? How did I get mixed up in all this?"

(Ah yes! you were forgetting about that!)

"You?"

The light brightened slightly.

"You, my poor lad, were an unexpected gift from providence for them: a saint. The way you took upon yourself all the sins of Commerce, shed the customers' tears for them and whipped up the hatred of every uneasy conscience in the Store, the extraordinary gift you have for attracting any stray arrows straight into your breast soon turned you into a saint in these ogres' eyes! As such, they wanted your hide. More than that, they wanted your halo, too! Sullying a real-life saint, having him convicted of murder, holding him up as the guilty party for public opprobrium was all rather tempting for such a gang of old devils, don't you think? The result was that they nearly had you lynched by your workmates. You remember how fortunate it was that Caregga was there . . ."

"But I'm not a fucking saint, for Christ's sake!"

"That will be up to the Vatican or, to be more precise, to the Congregation of Rites, in two or three centuries' time, if someone tries to have you canonized . . . Be that as it may, the last of our ogres went rather further than the other ones. Your friend Theo had obviously told him a lot about you, in his naïve, admiring way, and the fact that you are a big-brotherly defender of orphans unleashed his hatred. He saw you as another Saint Nicholas saving the innocents from the salting-tub. And the salting-tub was his property. He was the one who filled it up. You were, in a sense, taking the bread from out of his mouth. Here was a man who hated you as you will never be hated again. By tricking you into killing him right under the noses of the police, he was sure that you would be caught red-handed and that that would be the end of you. He even went so far as to put a charm on you beforehand. Because he really did put a charm on you the other night in the métro, didn't he?"

(He did.)

"Just imagine how thrilled he was when he saw that you were falling into his trap. He died convinced that we were going to pin six murders on you."

(. . .)

"What was his name?"

A mute stare. The light dimmed.

"There, my lad, you are on forbidden ground. He was, as they say, respectable."

(So you were right about that, Theo, my old mate . . .)

As a result, the conclusions of the inquiry would remain secret. There would be no more bombs going off in the Store. But Sainclair would replace the coppers with security guards, who would continue to frisk the customers so that the turnover would continue to rise. The security guards would play at guarding the Tomb to the Unknown Soldier. (And the most important thing for any unknown soldier is to be brimming with life.)

Two more details. When I asked Coudrier why he hadn't intervened, why he'd let me dive on that gorilla, he gave me a Charles-de-Gaulle answer. He said:

"It had to happen that way."

And, a little later, when he was showing me out the door:

"You were wrong to get yourself dismissed from the Store, Monsieur Malaussène. You made an excellent Scapegoat."

On the way out from the station, I hoped for a second that a lemon-yellow 4CV would be waiting for me, parked on a no-parking area. I felt an enormous need to romp in the valleys of its owner, then to fall asleep in her shade. Nothing doing. There was just the black hole of the métro. Too bad. It was going to be a Julia-less night. A Julius night.

Chapter 39

At home, various surprises were awaiting me. First off, a huge batch of job offers. Which I chucked in the bin as soon as I'd read them. Every company in the country was out to fatten itself up on the Scapegoat.

Not a chance. No way. "Nehver hergain", as a pope once said about a war.

The last of the envelopes came from the Ministry of Education. I opened it just to see how much the State wanted to pay me for getting trampled on in its name.

It wasn't going to pay me anything. What it wanted me to do was pay it for the damage done to Jeremy's school. The bill was enclosed.

I was still counting the noughts when the intercom crackled into life.

"Ben? Come down at once. There's a surprise for you."

So of course I bombed downstairs.

It was quite a big surprise. (It was even a double-big surprise!)

Mother! It was mother.

She was as pretty as a mother. She was still as young as a mother. And she was pregnant up to her neck, as only young pretty mothers can be.

I said:

"Mum! Mum!"

She said:

"Benjamin! My number one son!"

She tried to hug me in her arms, but the newcomer there on the inside was already getting in the way.

I said:

"Where's Robert?"

She answered:

"Robert's gone."

I pointed at the little sphere.

"And that?"

She answered:

"It's the last one, Ben. I promise you it is."

I picked up the phone and rang Queen Zabo.